'Will you kiss me?'

Paris lifted a hand to touch his face gently. Will froze, then raised a cynical eyebrow. 'For old times' sake?'

'No.' She shook her head. 'For now. For the me I am now.'

For a long moment Will didn't move and she thought that he was going to deny her, but his grip tightened on her arm and he drew her slowly towards him, his eyes holding hers. He lowered his head to hers, touched her lips with his mouth. For an instant it was as if time had stood still and he was kissing her for the very first time all over again.

Sally Wentworth was born and raised in Hertfordshire, where she still lives, and started writing after attending an evening class course. She is married and has one son. There is always a novel on the bedside table, but she also does craftwork, plays bridge, and is the president of a National Trust group. They go to the ballet and theatre regularly and to open-air concerts in the summer. Sometimes she doesn't know how she finds the time to write!

CHRISTMAS NIGHTS

BY
SALLY WENTWORTH

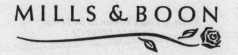

MILLS & BOON

*MILLS & BOON and the Rose Device
are trademarks of the publisher.
Harlequin Mills & Boon Limited,
Eton House, 18-24 Paradise Road, Richmond, Surrey TW9 1SR*

© Sally Wentworth 1996

ISBN 0 263 79825 9

*Set in Times Roman 10 on 11¼ pt.
94-9611-58188 C1*

*Printed and bound in Great Britain
by BPC Paperbacks Limited, Aylesbury*

CHAPTER ONE

PARIS had been home for less than an hour when the police came. The flat was cold and unwelcoming. When she'd left to go to Budapest six weeks ago the weather had been mild and autumnal and it hadn't seemed worthwhile leaving the heating on. Now, a week before Christmas, it was freezing outside and the flat was not much warmer.

She'd turned the heating up as high as it would go, drawn the curtains across the frosted windows, fixed herself a drink, and kicked off her shoes as she sat on the settee and began to go through the piles of letters, Christmas cards and junk mail that she had found on the doormat.

When the buzzer sounded Paris frowned, of half a mind to ignore it, but it rang imperatively for a second time, and with a sigh she went over to the entry phone. The faces of two men she didn't know looked at her from the screen.

'Yes?'

'Miss Paris Reid?'

'Yes.'

'We're policemen, Miss Reid.' The nearest man held up an identity card. 'May we talk to you, please?'

'Has there been an accident?' Paris asked, immediately fearful for her parents.

'No, it's nothing like that, but we need to talk to you urgently.'

'You'd better come up, then.'

She waited by the open door for the lift to arrive at her floor. The flat, in the northern suburbs of London, was her own, the mortgage paid for out of her quite considerable earnings. There was only one bedroom, but that suited Paris fine; she had no intention of ever sharing it with a female flatmate—or anyone else, if it came to that.

The policemen had said that there hadn't been an accident but Paris was still uneasy as she greeted them and led the way into her sitting-room. 'It isn't one of my parents?' she asked anxiously.

'No, Miss Reid. It's about Noel Ramsay.'

For a moment it didn't mean anything, then she grew still. 'Noel Ramsay?' she repeated, to give herself time.

'Yes. You must remember that you were on the jury when he was tried for murder, nearly four years ago now.'

'Yes, of course.' She dredged her memory. 'He escaped, didn't he? I seem to remember reading about it in the papers some months ago.'

'That's right.' The policeman who'd introduced himself as a detective inspector gave her a pleased smile, as if she were a bright pupil in a classroom.

'But why on earth should you come to me about him? You did catch him again, didn't you?'

'No, I'm afraid we didn't,' the inspector admitted ruefully. He paused, then said, 'I don't want to alarm you, but you may remember that at the trial Ramsay swore to be revenged on everyone who put him away.'

For a brief, horrible moment the vision of Ramsay's face, twisted by hate, shouting threats and abuse as he was dragged away, came sharply back into Paris's mind. 'Yes, I remember,' she said tightly.

'Yes. Well—I'm afraid it's beginning to look as if he's carrying out his threat.'

'What do you mean?'

'Haven't you been reading the papers lately? The barrister who prosecuted Ramsay was killed by a hit-and-run driver about three months ago, and then one of the policemen who arrested him was very badly injured when the brakes on his car failed—a newish car that had always been well maintained.'

'Couldn't those things have been coincidental?'

'Possibly.' The inspector shrugged. 'But a month ago one of the prosecution witnesses just disappeared, and then a member of the jury was found dead in suspicious circumstances. Two incidents could possibly be coincidence, but hardly four. And so we—' He broke off. 'Are you all right, Miss Reid?'

Every last vestige of colour had fled from Paris's face and her throat didn't seem to work. Her whole being felt suspended in time, too frozen to breathe, but by a tremendous effort of will-power she somehow forced herself to say, 'Which—which member of the jury?'

'A Mrs Sheila Rayner. She was the foreman of the jury, if you remember,' he answered, looking at her curiously.

'Yes, of course.' Paris's heart started to beat again, relief to flow through her veins and bring the colour back to her cheeks. 'That—that's terrible. I'm so sorry.' Getting to her feet, she turned away. 'Would you like a drink?' Both men refused but she topped up her own glass and took a long swallow before she faced them again. 'I didn't know any of this. I've been away, in Hungary, and it wasn't easy to get English papers.'

'We know,' the inspector said with a small smile. 'We've been calling here hoping to find you for a week or so.'

'To warn me?'

'Partly that, but also because we're taking everyone who was involved in the trial to a place of safety. We don't want anyone else being hurt while we catch Ramsay again.'

Paris's eyes widened. 'You're taking *everyone* involved? Even the jurors?'

'Everyone,' he confirmed. 'The judge, barristers, witnesses, jurors, even the clerk of the court.'

'But surely the jurors' names were never stated in court; how could Ramsay possibly know who we are?'

A grim look came into the policeman's eyes. 'Unfortunately the records of the case have disappeared from the archives; we can only assume that Ramsay or an accomplice must have taken them. And if he has—' he shrugged expressively '—then Ramsay knows the names and addresses of everyone connected with the trial.'

'Don't you have any leads?'

'We're pursuing the matter with the utmost urgency, of course,' he told her, in what was plainly a stock police phrase for saying that they didn't have a clue. 'But he's already got one of you jurors and I'm not taking any chances. So if you'll pack a suitcase we'll get you to a place of safety tonight.'

Paris stared at him unseeingly, her mind whirling as she tried to take in the implications, decide what to do. 'Are all the people being taken to the same place or are you splitting them up?'

'No, you'll all be together. It makes it easier to protect you that way.'

That, of course, made her mind up fast. 'I'm sorry,' she said firmly, 'but I can't possibly go. Please don't worry about me. I shall be quite safe here and I—'

'You will *not* be safe.'

He spoke sharply but Paris didn't hesitate before saying, 'But of course I will. My old address may be on the records but I've moved three times since then. And I'm ex-directory. No one could possibly trace me.'

'We did,' the second policeman, a sergeant, pointed out with some irony.

'Yes, but you're the police; with all the resources you have you're supposed to find people.'

'You're on the electoral roll for this district. Anyone can walk into a library, look at it, and find your address. With a Christian name like yours it was simple.'

Paris bit her lip, not for the first time blaming her parents for giving her such a distinctive name. But she persisted, saying, 'I'm sorry, but I refuse to go. You can't make me.'

'No, we can't,' the inspector agreed. 'Is it because you've made plans for Christmas, or are you having guests to stay?'

'No,' she admitted. 'But I've already been away for over a month; there's loads I have to catch up on, at work as well as here.'

'I've already spoken to your employers and they quite understand the situation. They told me to tell you that they don't expect to see you again until Ramsay is caught.'

She gasped, amazed that the police had gone to those lengths before they'd even talked to her. 'I've been invited to several parties,' she said doggedly. 'If I didn't go to them my friends would worry and—'

'In that case you can phone and tell them you've changed your plans. Tell them you've had an unexpected invitation and that you'll be going away for Christmas instead.'

'But...' She sought for a convincing argument. 'But it could take weeks, months even, before you catch him. I can't possibly be away for that length of time.'

'We don't anticipate it taking anything like that long, miss.'

'Are you saying that you're close to catching Ramsay?'

'I don't want to commit myself, but just take my word for it that it won't be for very long.'

Paris didn't believe him but there was no point in saying so. Finishing her drink, she shoved her hands into the pockets of her jacket so that the men couldn't see the way they tightened into fists. 'Look,' she began, then stopped, not wanting to say this. But there was no help for it—the policemen were so very determined. 'There are reasons—very personal reasons—why I can't possibly go with you.'

'What reasons?'

'They needn't concern you,' she snapped. 'But I am *not* going.'

The middle-aged inspector, who looked as if he wouldn't be sorry when retirement came along, gave her a tight-lipped look. 'Very well, Miss Reid. In that case you leave me no choice.'

'What do you mean?' Paris asked warily.

'If you won't let us take you to a place of safety, then I shall have to give you police protection.'

To Paris that didn't sound at all bad but his voice had had a threatening note in it, so she said, 'Which means?'

'A woman police officer will have to be with you at all times, day and night, and there will also be a male constable at your door. We will turn this place into a fortress,' he threatened determinedly.

'But my neighbours would hate that—and besides, there isn't enough room here for two people to live,' Paris protested.

'No help for it, I'm afraid—if you're going to be obstinate.'

He had deliberately made the conditions impossible to accept, she realised, and burst out on a desperate note, 'Don't people's personal feelings matter to you?'

'Not when their lives are in danger, no. I can't let them matter,' the inspector answered emphatically.

She was cornered, and hesitated, wondering whether to throw herself on his mercy and explain just why it was impossible for her to go. But a glance at the inspector's set face, wearily patient but determined, made her decide it would be no use. He was too stolid to understand the trauma of seeing again an ex-lover, a man who had, quite literally, thrown her out of his life.

Clenching her fists till it hurt, Paris said, 'Are the other people already at this safe place?'

'Yes.'

'All of them? All the jurors?'

His assessing eyes met hers. 'All except the lady who was murdered, yes.'

Murdered. Such a dreadful word. It brought home to Paris for the first time the danger she was in. But she still said, 'Please, I can't go with—with all the others. I'll go somewhere else, if you like, but not with them.'

He nodded, in no way surprised. 'I see.'

She caught her breath, realising that there had been no need for any soul-searching; he already knew it all. 'Yes, very likely you do,' Paris said bitterly.

The inspector glanced at his colleague, hesitated, then said with a degree of sympathy that she hadn't expected, and which confirmed his knowledge, 'It probably won't be for long, perhaps just a week or so, and then you'll be able to come home. There will be a lot of people there, enough so you won't be thrown together with anyone you don't want to be with. You'll have your own room and be as private as you like. But I'm sorry, I can't arrange for somewhere else for you at this short notice. If it goes on for longer I might be able to arrange for you to go somewhere else after Christmas, though.'

When it would be a complete waste of time, Paris thought despondently. Her nightmare of the last three years had been that she might chance to meet the man she'd been so in love with, have to face him again and see the contempt in his eyes. Now it looked as if she was not only going to see him, but would have to spend an indefinite period in his proximity.

With a sigh, Paris said dully, 'If you'll promise to find me somewhere else as soon as possible, then, all right, I'll come. Where are we going?'

'I'm afraid we're not allowed to tell you that.'

She gave him a look that spoke volumes. 'I am going to wash my hair,' she said forcefully. 'And then I'm going to have something to eat, unpack, and make several phone calls. *Then* I'll get ready to go. Is that all right by you?' Her hands were on her hips and the last sentence was said in a dangerous tone that dared him to argue.

The inspector, having got his own way by forceful coercion, could have been magnanimous, but all he said was, 'So long as you can do all that within the next two hours, yes.'

They took her in a car and drove for quite some way, but then, to Paris's surprise, the car stopped and they hurried her into a station and onto a train where she was to share a sleeping compartment with a policewoman. The blinds were pulled down across the windows on both sides and she couldn't see out. The door was locked and the light turned low.

Paris's thoughts were far too full for her to want to sit and chat with the policewoman, so she said that she was tired, took off her shoes and coat and climbed into the upper bunk, firmly closing her eyes.

Her heart was filled with a dread so deep that it was almost like a physical fear. How would she bear it if Will openly showed his hatred of her? Even now, after so long, it was still sometimes hard to understand how it had all gone so wrong—so horribly, humiliatingly wrong. Maybe it was because of the circumstances in which they'd met: at a murder trial, of all things. But there had been such radiant happiness, too, at the beginning...

The train journeyed on through the night, swaying, clanking along the rails, the rushing air loud outside, and Paris's mind went back to the very beginning, when she had been sitting at breakfast with Emma, one morning in late spring.

'Jury service!' Paris gazed at the letter in her hand in consternation. 'But I can't possibly do it. I don't have the time.'

'When are you supposed to go?' Emma, her flatmate, reached over and took the letter from her. 'The seventh. That's only three weeks away. And at the Old Bailey, too; that's where they have the longest cases, isn't it?'

Paris's frown deepened into gloom. 'I know—and I'm supposed to be going to the conference in Brussels that week.'

'Perhaps you can get out of it,' Emma suggested languidly as she handed the letter back. 'Tell them you're going on holiday or something.'

Paris hesitated. 'Wouldn't that be against the law? Couldn't you be fined or something if you were found out?'

Emma gave an astonished laugh. 'For heaven's sake! Who's going to find out? People do it all the time.'

'Well, I can try, I suppose,' Paris said, still rather dubious, but she reflected that Emma, who was more than ten years older and worked for the same company, usually knew what she was talking about.

Later that morning, as soon as she arrived at her office at the cable network company for which she worked as a sales representative, Paris called the clerk of the court's office and asked to be released from doing the jury service. He asked for proof that she had booked a holiday, and when she lamely admitted that she had none he refused point-blank to let her off.

'Isn't it possible to postpone it indefinitely?' she begged.

'No, madam, it is not,' the man said shortly.

So there was no getting out of it. Paris had to go and see her boss, who arranged for Emma to attend the Brussels conference in her place. Paris was furious at her bad luck; she'd had this job for less than a year since leaving university and was putting everything she had into it. Representing the company at conferences, going abroad to promote their network strategies, being always available to visit potential clients constituted a big part of the job.

Paris had passed the training course with flying colours, was one of the brightest young reps, and knew that a good career lay ahead of her. Which she certainly intended to achieve. She was ambitious and wanted to get to the top just as soon as she possibly could. But there were always others with the same ambitions, the same aims. Having to sit through some criminal case for weeks on end, or even months, she thought with a groan, wouldn't do her career any good at all.

Angrily reluctant to serve as she was, Paris had to admit to a feeling of awe when she arrived at the Central Criminal Court—the Old Bailey as the building was commonly known—in the heart of the City of London. The courtroom was so old, the polished wooden benches and the judge's throne-like seat high on a dais so reminiscent of all the trial films she'd ever seen that she couldn't help but feel the solemnity and power of the place. Looking at the dock, she thought of all the people who had been tried there—murderers, rapists; she gave a shiver, her anger momentarily chastened.

Her fellow jurors seemed to have similar feelings. Earlier, they'd had to stand one by one and give their name and age and take the oath. Paris hated that, considering her age to be her own business. When it was her turn, her voice had a strong note of defiance as she said, 'Paris Reid. I'm twenty-two.'

A couple of the younger barristers smiled, as did one of the male jurors, she noticed. He was sitting on the end of the row and hadn't yet been called—a dark-haired man with a strong jaw and clean-cut features adding up to a good-looking face. He was the last to take the oath and did so in a firm voice.

'William Alexander Brydon. Twenty-nine. I swear by Almighty God that I will faithfully try the defendant and true verdict give according to the evidence.'

The oath, which Paris had hardly taken in, sounded very impressive when spoken in his deep, attractive tone, making her realise again the solemnity of the court. The judge must have been impressed too, because when he asked them to choose a foreman from amongst themselves he looked straight at William Brydon. But before the latter could speak a middle-aged woman stood up purposefully and volunteered herself, which pleased Paris; she was all for women sticking up for their rights. The judge merely raised his eyebrows slightly.

The case they were to hear was one of aggravated assault and murder. The prisoner, a man in his early forties named Noel Ramsay, was accused of beating up several people, one of whom—a man who had tried to steal Ramsay's girlfriend—had later died. The man in the dock was smartly dressed, had a boyishly good-looking face and a figure that was only just beginning to run to fat.

Paris found it difficult to imagine him hurting anyone. Perhaps it was the engaging, crinkly-eyed smile that he flashed at them all, the look of surprised innocence in his eyes, as if he still couldn't believe that he was there, that it was all happening to him.

That first morning it seemed to be all technical stuff. They broke for lunch, most of which time Paris spent on the phone, first to her office, trying to keep up with everything that was happening, and then to customers. She had just a few minutes left in which to grab a couple of bites from a sandwich before it was time to go back into the courtroom.

The jurors automatically sat in the same places as before. That afternoon they listened to a pathologist and had to look at photographs that made Paris's stomach turn over. If she hadn't really been aware of the seriousness of the case before, she certainly was after that.

At the end of the day, Paris rushed out of the building and drove to her office in a town to the north of London. There she spent three hours at her desk before driving home to a scratch supper and bed. She was young and healthy and could keep up the hectic pace for a while, but during the second week she began to feel the pressure. To add to everything the unpredictable English weather decided to have an early heatwave.

Paris overslept one morning and arrived just as the jurors were filing into their places. She gave a hasty apology to the clerk of the court, a man moved up for her, and she slipped in at the end of the row. Because she'd been so busy she had hardly talked to her fellow jurors and it took her a minute before she remembered that her neighbour's name was William Brydon. He gave her an amused smile which she met with a small shrug.

The evidence that morning was again technical. There was no air-conditioning in the court and it was very hot. The barristers were sweltering under their white wigs and several members of the jury took off their jackets.

Paris tried to concentrate but found her eyes drooping. She straightened in her seat, licked dry lips and wished she could have a drink. The police witness droned on—something about makes of cars that the accused had owned and sold. William Brydon's shoulder was invitingly close. Paris's head rested gently on it and she fell asleep.

'She seems to have fainted, my lord.'

The words, spoken loudly close by in a man's voice, woke her.

Paris blinked, came to guiltily, and would have jerked upright, but William Brydon was gently slapping at her cheeks, leaning over her so that she was hidden from everyone else. 'You fainted,' he murmured so that only she could hear. 'You don't want them to restart the whole trial, do you?' he added insistently.

Realising what he was doing, Paris gratefully fell in with the act. She gave a realistic moan and let him put her head down between her knees—none too gently, she noticed. The clerk and the woman foreman of the jury came over, the latter with some smelling salts which she insisted on holding under Paris's nose, making her sneeze.

'Perhaps if she could have some fresh air?' William Brydon suggested.

'We'll adjourn the court for lunch,' the judge decided.

Putting a strong arm round her, her neighbour escorted her out of the court, down the long corridor and out into the street. Not far away there was a small green oasis of trees surrounding the remains of a ruined church. When they reached its screening shade he immediately withdrew his arm. 'A heavy date last night?' he asked sardonically.

'No, I was working,' she retorted indignantly.

'After a day here? Are you self-employed or something?'

'No, I work for a cable network company. I'm a sales rep.'

Again his mouth, the lower lip fuller than the other, twisted with irony. 'Can't they manage without you?'

Paris's face hardened. 'I want to make sure they don't find out that they can,' she said shortly, adding, in a voice as scathing as his had been, 'You obviously don't have to worry about your job—if you have one.'

He looked amused. 'Oh, I have one. I'm a financial consultant, here in the City.'

Paris said moodily, 'Right now I should be in Brussels, representing my company at a medical conference, trying to persuade television and telephone companies to use our networks. It was to be my first time alone. And instead I'm stuck with this case. It's all so slow. And it could go on for weeks.'

'It might at that,' he agreed. 'So we'll just have to make the best of it, won't we?'

There was something in his voice, a note that immediately made her realise he was aware of her as a woman. Glancing quickly up at him, Paris saw that he was looking her over, from her short red-gold hair, down her slim figure, to her legs beneath the fashionably short skirt. 'Seen enough?' she said with a tilt of her chin, but not at all displeased.

He grinned. 'For now. My name's Will, by the way. Will Brydon.'

She smiled and shook the hand he held out to her. 'Mine's Paris Reid.'

'Yes, I know. An unusual name.'

'My parents went to Paris for a holiday; I was the result.' They began to stroll under the shade of the trees and she said, 'Thanks for helping me back there. I suppose I would have got into terrible trouble if they'd found out I'd fallen asleep. It's rather like being back at school with the teacher watching you all the time.'

They came to an ice-cream cart and Will bought her a cornet—one with a chocolate flake stuck into it. Paris ate it delicately, trailing her tongue along the chocolate, scooping a little of the ice cream and raising it to her mouth.

Will slowed as he openly watched her. 'You know,' he said with a sigh, 'you have the sexiest way of eating an ice.'

She laughed, her face lighting up. Glancing at him, she liked what she saw. His eyes were grey, clear and intelligent, under dark brows, the left one of which had a slight quirk, as if he raised it more than the other. His bone structure was good, his cheekbones high above the clean jawline, and there was a humorous look to his mouth.

He was tall, too—a definite plus in Paris's eyes because she was tall herself. Walking with him, she had to look up at him, which put him at about six feet two or three, she guessed. Perhaps it was his height that gave him such physical self-assurance, but there was an irresistible magnetism about him, as if he was full of energy that he could hardly contain.

'Don't you find having to do this jury service a bind?' she asked him.

'In some ways, of course, but I find the whole process of the law fascinating to watch; there's so much history behind it all. It's something that I'll probably have to do only once in a lifetime so I want to do it to the best of my ability. And I suppose we should be grateful that we don't live in a police state where there is no jury system.'

Paris wrinkled her nose at him. 'That sounds terribly po-faced. Is that really what you think?'

Will laughed. 'I think it's a damn nuisance, but I may as well get it over and done with.'

'That's better. I'm not looking forward to having to reach a verdict, are you? Suppose we don't all agree and have to stay in a hotel or something for days.' She looked at him from under her lashes. 'Your wife—or partner—would probably hate that.'

Will's lips curled in amusement. 'Fortunately I have neither, so there's no problem. But maybe you do?'

Paris shook her head. 'No, I'm single and unattached.' She added, 'At the moment,' to let him know that she wasn't hard up for boyfriends.

'Well, I'm glad that I've met you "at the moment",' Will remarked, and they both laughed. His eyes on her, he said, 'Maybe you'd better sit next to me when we go back in the court-room. Just to make sure you don't go to sleep again, of course.'

'Of course,' Paris agreed demurely. And as they walked back to the court they both knew that this could be the start of a very interesting friendship.

Emma came back from Brussels and told her off for trying to fit in her job with the trial. 'You can't possibly go on like this,' she remonstrated. 'Look, give me your customer list and I'll look after them for you until you're back at the office,' she offered.

'Oh, Emma, would you? It is rather getting me down,' Paris said gratefully.

Emma's kindness made Paris once again think herself extremely lucky that the older woman had taken a liking to her and more or less taken her under her wing. Her own parents had split up many years ago and both had remarried, but Paris didn't really feel at home with either of them, although they both always made her welcome and tried to include her in their new families.

When she'd first joined the company she'd lived in a bedsit quite nearby, but then Emma had become friendly with her and finally asked her if she'd like to share her flat. 'It's in the suburbs of London, mind,' Emma warned her. 'You'd have to drive into the office every day.'

But Paris hadn't minded that at all; the company had given her a car and the thought of living in London excited her.

At first, because of the difference in their ages, she'd been surprised that Emma had been so friendly, but she'd also been flattered by it too. Emma had quite a senior position in the sales department; it was her job to oversee and train the new recruits and to stand in when an emergency occurred, as in the case of the Brussels conference.

Because she was mostly based at head office, Emma was no longer entitled to a company car, and it didn't take Paris long to work out that one of the reasons why Emma had offered to let her share the flat was so that she could get a lift to and from work every day. But Paris was so grateful to her that she didn't mind in the least. And she was grateful to her again, now, for taking on her workload, especially now that she'd met Will and realised how pleasantly her lunch-hours could be if spent in his company instead of on the phone.

The heatwave continued and she and Will got into the habit of taking their sandwiches out to the old churchyard, where they sat on the grass beneath the trees to eat and talk. They talked as strangers do, telling each other about themselves, their likes and dislikes, asking questions, getting to know one another, until they weren't strangers any longer.

Instead of being reluctant to go to the court, Paris became eager to get there. She took care with her appearance and felt a thrill of pleasure when Will's grey eyes went over her admiringly. And he was so goodlooking himself that she enjoyed being seen with him, liked walking along with him beside her, so tall and broad that he made her feel delicately feminine in comparison. From having lunch together, it took very little time before Will asked her to stay behind in town one evening and have dinner with him.

They went to see a film first, and afterwards had dinner at Topo Gigio—'The best Italian restaurant in Soho,' Will declared. He seemed very familiar with London—had lived there all his life, he told her, except for his years at university.

Paris envied him that; she had fallen in love with the city, with its pace and constant change, with its shops, cinemas and theatres. In London you got everything first—the new films and new fashions—and met people who were as ambitious as she was herself, and men who were eager to take out a pretty girl like Paris.

So there had been a lot of dates, but Will was the first man—the first real man, not someone of her own age— that Paris felt strongly attracted to.

After that first dinner date he insisted on taking her home in a cab, which must have cost the earth, and kept it waiting when he walked her to her door where he leant her against the wall, put his hands on her shoulders, and bent to kiss her. He merely touched her lips gently with his at first—small kisses that explored her mouth.

Paris, who wasn't that experienced, had been brainwashed by a thousand films and books and some equally inexperienced boyfriends into thinking that passionate clinches and devouring kisses were the bee's knees. But she found this light exploration, the soft, teasing kisses, both tantalising and sensuous. His breath was warm and she could smell the faint tang of aftershave that still clung to his skin.

It came to her that he was a very masculine kind of man, with a powerful aura of sensuality that excited her. He was the kind of man who knew what he wanted. And right now he wanted her.

Resting her hands against his chest, Paris closed her eyes. Opening her mouth, she felt him touch the tip of her tongue—a brief touch that she found incredibly erotic. She gave an involuntary sound of pleasure and Will's hands tightened a little on her shoulders.

Raising her hand, she caressed the back of his neck, his hair silky under her fingers, and she felt him give a small sigh as his hand came down to her waist and drew her against him. His kiss deepened, taking all her mouth, but it was still gentle, and she responded willingly.

It was a while before Will straightened. Pushing back his thick dark hair, he looked down at her with the heaviness of desire in his eyes, but then he gave a crooked grin. 'I think maybe I'd better go.'

'Mmm. Your taxi is waiting.'

But he bent to kiss her again before he drew away for a second time and said, 'See you in court.'

Then he waved and was gone, leaving Paris with an overwhelming feeling of physical excitement and a longing for him to kiss her again.

That kiss marked a new awareness of each other and was the start of an inevitable closeness between them. But just as Will had been in no hurry with that first kiss so they were in no hurry to become even closer, both of them recognising that this was something special and wanting to anticipate each phase of their relationship. Maybe Paris would have been more eager, but it was Will who set the pace, he who had the dominant role.

They didn't go out every night; Will worked out at a gym two nights a week and also spent time in his own office, but they were together with increasing frequency.

The trial lasted over a month and was drawing to its close. Although they talked a lot to each other, they seldom discussed the trial. It was bad enough having to listen to all the terrible details during the day without thinking about it during their time alone together. They wanted to put it out of their minds, to escape from it. But at last, on a Thursday, it came to the judge's summing-up, which lasted nearly a whole day. The judge was eminently fair, pointing out facts that they should remember, think about, but emphasising that they had heard everything and it was up to them to make up their minds now.

Leaving the court and going into the jury-room felt strange. They had used the room so many times before, but now they had come to make the decision, to give their verdict, to condemn a man to prison or to set him free. All twelve of them, without exception, felt the burden heavy on their shoulders.

They didn't all agree on all the counts the first time, which meant that they all had to spend the night in a hotel, closed off from their homes and families—twelve special people with an enormous responsibility.

A table had been set aside for them in the hotel restaurant and they ate together, but afterwards they were free, within limits, to do as they liked. Four of them began to play cards, others went to their rooms, and some to the bar. Paris and Will were among the latter, but they sat in a corner, apart from the others, who gave them indulgent looks.

The kisses they had exchanged had got hotter over the past weeks, and both of them were experiencing deep frustration, which was heightened by sitting next to each other every day in court and having to pretend that there was nothing between them. Their hands, hidden by the bench in front of them, had often touched, their knees brushed and not always by accident, but they hadn't dared to look directly at one another in case they gave themselves away to the beady-eyed judge. This secretiveness had added spice to their romance, but now it was coming to an end.

Nothing had been said, but both of them were awaiting the end of the court case with eager, excited anticipation. It was as if they had tacitly agreed that a man's trial was an entirely wrong background against which to form a relationship, and that they couldn't take their affair further until it was over, until they were free of it. And now that time was almost here.

'Hopefully we'll reach a verdict tomorrow and we won't have to stay here over the weekend,' Will remarked. His eyes, darkening a little, rested on her face. 'So, if we're free, will you come away with me for the weekend?'

'Away?' Paris felt her colour heighten. 'Where—where to?'

Will gave a sudden, almost rueful grin. 'I haven't really thought that far. All I can think of is being with you,' he admitted. 'Where would you like to go?'

Her blush deepened at his admission, but Paris said, 'I don't know. In the country somewhere, I suppose. You said you could ride a horse; how about teaching me?'

'Definitely not,' Will said positively.

'Why not?'

'You might get bruised and stiff. I think we should do something very, very gentle—during the day.' His eyes met hers, smiling and suggestive, promising so much.

Her voice strangely husky, and somehow knowing that he would make a good lover, Paris said, 'So what do you recommend?'

'Painting, archery. Or why don't we just play it by ear?'

'All right.' Her voice shook a little. 'We'll do that, then.'

Reaching out, Will took her hand and raised it to his lips. 'Thank you, my darling.'

It was quite late on Friday afternoon before the jury finally reached a verdict. Paris gave an inner sigh of relief when it was decided at last. All day she had been on tenterhooks in case they lost their weekend together. Will, she knew, had felt the same. Their eyes had often met in exasperation and impatience; to them the verdict was cut and dried and it had been frustrating, to say the least, waiting for everyone else to agree.

They filed back into court, the judge came in and they were asked if they had reached a verdict. The foreman replied that they had and the prisoner stood up. He was a little pale, Paris saw, but there was still a jauntiness in his shoulders, the charming smile clung to his lips, and it came to her that he had the inescapable belief that they would acquit him.

When the verdicts were read out Ramsay changed completely. For a few moments he just stared as if he couldn't believe his ears. Then he shouted, 'No!' and grasped the front of the box.

The policemen on either side of him quietened him as the judge gave sentence. 'You are an evil and sadistic man, entirely unable to control your emotions, and your vindictiveness finally led to murder. I sentence you to life imprisonment.'

'No!' the prisoner shouted again. His face convulsed with fury. The boyish charm disappeared and his inherent cruelty was plain to see as he shouted, 'I'll get you for this. All of you!' His frenzied eyes swept round the court. 'Every last one of you.' His finger stabbed out like a stiletto blade at the judge, the officials and then the jury. 'Curse you, you filthy swine. I'll make you pay. I'll cut your throats. I'll make you beg to die.'

He went on swearing and screaming insults as the guards tried to overpower him and eventually managed to drag him out of the dock and down out of the court. When they'd gone and the door had banged after him, there was a terrible silence, everyone too shocked by Ramsay's hatred and venom to move or speak. It was the judge who broke it.

Wryly, speaking from long experience, he said, 'You must take no notice of his threats. You have done your duty and I will make it my concern to see that you are all exempted from further jury service for the next ten years. Thank you for your services. You may now leave the court.'

They did so numbly, as did everyone else: the judge, the barristers and clerks, the public up in the gallery, their ears still ringing with the curses that had been hurled at them.

Will collected his car from a nearby car park and drove Paris to her flat where she packed some clothes for the weekend, then to his place where he threw some things into a bag. Within an hour they were on the road and heading out of London, away from the court and the evils they'd had to listen to for the past month or so, away from the threats and curses that had shattered their peace.

It was quite late before they reached the country hotel where Will had booked a room for the weekend. There was no time even to look around; they were shown to their room and Paris took the bathroom first, showering and changing quickly. Then it was Will's turn, and immediately he was ready they went down to the dining-room for dinner.

Here, at last, they were able to relax, to enjoy a meal after having had little to eat all day, to drink a bottle of wine which helped to dispel the slight embarrassment that had been forced on them when they'd had to rush to change in each other's presence but when they weren't intimate enough for that yet. The meal also helped to ease the tension that Noel Ramsay's outburst had caused.

As Will said, they had more pleasant things to think about.

Looking into his eyes, so warm and expressive, Paris felt her heart miss a beat then fill with the excitement of anticipation, an emotion mirrored in his gaze. 'What things?' she asked, being deliberately provocative.

He gave a slow smile. 'Do you really want me to tell you here and now?'

Again her heart leaped. 'Yes,' she said on an unsteady note.

'All right.' Taking her hand, he lifted it to his lips and kissed her fingers one by one. 'We could think of how I'm going to very slowly take off all your clothes and look at you and then tell you how beautiful you are. And about the way I'm going to carry on kissing you like this until there won't be a part of your body that I haven't touched and loved. And of how—'

Paris hastily reached out and put her fingers against his lips, silencing him. 'Don't,' she breathed, her eyes wide with awareness, her cheeks flushed. 'You mustn't.'

'Oh, but I must tell you how lovely you are, my darling.'

'No, I meant...'

'What? What did you mean?'

Her colour deepened and she looked suddenly shy. 'I meant that you mustn't make me feel this way—not here, in public.'

His grip on her hand tightened a little. 'Tell me how I make you feel.'

She hesitated, then said, 'So—wanton.'

Will smiled, the pleasure at her answer deep in his eyes. But he said warmly, 'And wanted too, my lovely one. You know that.'

'Yes.' Not trying to hide the desire she felt, she said, 'I feel that way too.' And, lowering her free hand below the table, she placed it on his thigh.

He gave a small gasp, her gesture completely unexpected, but then he laughed softly. 'Now who's turning who on?' Putting his hand over hers, he pressed it against himself, then said on a note of strong urgency, 'Let's go to bed.'

Paris gave him a demure look. 'You haven't finished your coffee.'

'To hell with the coffee,' he said emphatically.

His vehemence increased Paris's excitement; for someone who had been content to take things slowly up to now, he was showing a gratifying eagerness. Slipping her hand from under his, she picked up her own coffee-cup. 'Really? I'm quite thirsty,' she said teasingly. And she took a deliberately casual drink.

An answering gleam came into Will's eyes and he looked around as if searching for a waiter. 'You'll probably want another cup, then. And perhaps a liqueur. And then we might as well have—'

He broke off as Paris put her hand on his arm. She looked at him for a moment, then shook her head. 'No,' she said softly but with firmness. 'I want you to take me to bed.'

Will's grey eyes filled with warmth and desire. He didn't ask if she was sure, didn't fuss; he merely stood up and drew her to her feet with him. They said goodnight to the waiter and he tucked her arm in his, keeping hold of her hand as they walked across to the stairs and up to their room.

He had said what he wanted to do, what he intended to do, and he did start by undressing her slowly, murmuring words of pleasure at her beauty, his lips caressing her skin as he did so. But Paris was shaking with awareness, her breath coming in unsteady gasps that caught in her throat, her hands gripping his shoulders as he bent before her to take off her stockings.

Her pleasure and anticipation were an aphrodisiac too powerful for him to resist; Will's own breathing quickened and he stood to kiss her fiercely, saying her name over and over against her lips. 'Paris. Oh, Paris. I want you! Oh, God, I want you.'

The rest of her clothes came off fast, Will's soon joining the scattered heap on the floor. And then she was lying in the bed and there was no time to look, no time for endearments. She was reaching out to him, her body opening for him eagerly.

The next moment he was over her, taking her with overwhelming passion, lifting her towards the thrust of his body, and groaning out his climactic pleasure. He carried her with him, lifting her to spiralling excitement, to gasping, crying physical fulfilment, and then into the long aftermath of exhausted peace.

Earlier Will had ordered a bottle of champagne to be sent up to the room. It stood resplendent in its ice-bucket, but they hadn't even noticed it. When they'd recovered a little, when Will had kissed her lingeringly and told her how wonderful she was, he noticed the wine and laughed ruefully. 'The champagne was supposed to come before, not after.'

'Were you going to seduce me with it?' Paris asked, kissing his shoulder.

'It was in case we needed it,' he admitted.

'Idiot.' She licked his tiny nipple and was amazed to see it harden.

'Hey,' he said, bending to kiss her eyes. 'Have mercy.'

She laughed and reached up to caress his cheek with the back of her fingers. 'I'm glad we didn't have a big seduction scene. It was so good as it was.'

'And will be again, I hope.'

'Oh, I *know* it will,' she said, so emphatically that Will laughed.

'You're an amazing girl, you know that?'

'Why, thank you, kind sir.' She sat up and pulled the sheet up over her breasts. 'Why don't you open the champagne now?'

'Not if you're going to cover yourself like that,' Will said positively. Reaching over, he jerked the sheet from her hold and pulled it down again. 'This, my darling, is no time for prudery. And besides,' he added, his voice thickening, 'you're much too gorgeous to hide yourself away.'

Kneeling up, he cupped her breasts in his hands, his mouth slowly parting with concentration and growing concupiscence as he watched the rose hue of the areolae darken and the nipples thrust against his exploring fingers. 'Look how beautiful you are,' he murmured thickly, his eyes wide with reawakened desire. 'Can you wonder that I can't resist you? Look. Look for yourself.'

Slowly, with almost reluctant shyness, Paris lowered her eyes to look at her breasts. His hands, his skin dark against the whiteness of hers, held her tenderly. Her breasts had the firm elasticity of youth, were still small and perfect, and yet they seemed to fill his hands, to fit them perfectly.

As she watched, fascinated now, he moved his thumbs to circle gently the tender area around her nipples, touching nerve-ends, sending fires of frustration deep into her body. She had heard of eroticism, knew that these were among the most sensitive parts of her womanhood, but she had never known such sensual delight as she felt now.

To watch him toying with her, to feel the growing need inside her, to let her panting breath become a long groan of frustration, and to know from the tension in his hands and the sweat on his skin that Will felt the same way was the most exquisitely sexy moment she had ever known.

Still kneeling, as if in adoration, Will bent to kiss her breasts, sending shock waves of sensuality pulsing through her. Throwing back her head, Paris let out a low, animal moan of tormented pleasure. Coming up on her own knees, she held his head against her, crying out with the wonder of it.

Will at last lifted his head and looked at her, his breath an unsteady, panting groan of almost uncontrolled expectation. Paris's face was flushed with heat, her mouth parted and her lips trembling, her eyes great green pools of eager desire.

'Paris.'

He said her name again on a note of wonder but she mistook it for a question and said, 'Yes. Oh, yes, yes!'

Putting his hands on her hips, he drew her towards him, onto his lap, onto his manhood. She let out a great cry and put her arms round him, wanting to be closer and yet closer still, wanting to be a part of him, to take the intense pleasure he gave her and to give in return.

Afterwards they slept exhaustedly, tangled in the sheets, their arms around one another. During the night Will woke her with kisses and they made love again, so that it wasn't until the morning that they finally got round to opening the champagne and had it with breakfast instead.

CHAPTER TWO

PARIS and Will returned to London on Sunday evening, parting reluctantly outside her flat. Their weekend of love, of satiated sexuality was still in the glow in her eyes, in her flushed cheeks. Emma saw it and recognised it at once.

Her finely arched brows rose. 'Don't tell me you've been considering your verdict all this time?'

'No, we reached a decision on Friday. I've—er—been away.'

'With a man, obviously.'

'Yes,' Paris admitted, unable to keep from smiling.

Emma looked amused. 'So what was the verdict?'

'Guilty on all counts.'

'I meant on the man.'

'Oh.' Paris glowed. 'Marvellous! Fantastic! *Incredible.*'

'Good heavens! This man I've got to meet.'

There was a slight edge to Emma's voice, but Paris was too happy to notice it. 'And I want you to meet him; I'm sure you'll like each other,' she said with happy optimism.

She was still happy the next day when she went back to the office, eager to resume her interrupted career. Will was due to work out at the gym that evening and she had lots of chores to catch up on, so they'd agreed not to meet, but they might just as well have done because they spent ages on the phone, already missing each other, whispering words of intimacy that tantalised them both.

The next evening Will came to collect her and she introduced him to Emma, confident that they would like each other. Emma was friendly enough—very friendly really, making Will welcome and telling him, with that amused little smile she had, how Paris had described him. 'So of course I've been really looking forward to meeting a man with all these incredible attributes,' she finished.

But Will only gave her a polite smile that didn't reach his eyes, refused a drink and asked Paris if she was ready to leave.

'What did you tell her about me?' he asked as soon as they were outside.

'Only that I thought you were wonderful,' Paris admitted. 'I didn't go into details, if that's what you're thinking.'

'She certainly made it sound as if you had.'

'Emma was probably teasing you. I wouldn't tell anyone. You should know that.' She put her arm through his and lifted a glowing face. 'It's very, very special to me.'

Will smiled at that and kissed her, so she knew it was all right, but it was obvious that he didn't like Emma.

They didn't go out, instead spending the evening at his flat. Even though they had spent most of the previous weekend making love, it was still novel, still overwhelmingly exciting. Paris felt no shyness now as she undressed Will, doing it slowly, touching and kissing him, running her hands over his broad, smooth chest, along the muscles in his upper arms, so powerful, so male.

His waist was slim and his stomach had the tautness of an athlete's even when relaxed. But it tightened even more under her exploring fingers; she could feel the tension running through his body, the slow dew of expectation on his skin, hear the quickened beat of his heart. Paris let her hands move on in their exploration, stroking, caressing, until his arousal was complete and Will groaned with pleasure.

He would have taken her in his arms then, but she made him sit on a chair and watch as she took off her own clothes, doing so as coquettishly as she could imagine, watching with growing excitement as he gripped the edge of the chair until his knuckles showed white and he strove to control his need for her, then giving a cry of delight when he could stand it no longer and surged up to grab her and carry her to the bed in one long, eager stride.

Later, Will dragged himself from the bed, dressed, and went out for a Chinese take-away, which took a long time to eat because they kept stopping to kiss and, as Paris was wearing only a bathrobe, quite a lot of caressing went on as well. So it was inevitable that they just pushed the plates away and made love all over again.

Paris was on cloud nine hundred and ninety-nine, but they became rain clouds only a few days later. It was at work that things started to go wrong. During her time with the company Paris had worked hard to find new markets for their products and there were three new accounts that she was particularly proud to have won, having spent a great deal of time and effort in acquiring them.

They were, of course, among the accounts that Emma had been watching over for her during the trial, but when Paris went to contact the companies to tell them that she was back she was informed that they preferred to deal with Emma in future.

When Paris questioned her, Emma was most apologetic. 'Oh, dear, did they really say that? I kept in contact with them as you asked and I *was* able to help them over some queries they had. In fact I had to visit all three of the companies to sort out the problems.'

'Problems? There weren't any problems.'

'Well, they must have cropped up recently,' Emma said with a vague wave of her hand. 'But luckily I knew everything about the network systems involved so I was able to reassure them quickly. I thought that was what you would have wanted, Paris.'

'Well, yes, of course, but—'

'Maybe they realised I was more experienced,' Emma suggested. 'They're new accounts; perhaps it gave them more confidence to deal with someone older. Why don't you talk to the people involved, explain the situation?' she suggested. 'Although, of course, buyers do like to deal with just one person, not be messed around.' She gave a worried frown. 'We don't want to lose the accounts, do we? If we did, the sales director would definitely want to know why. But you must go ahead and explain things to them, of course.'

'No, as you said, we don't want to lose them,' Paris said slowly, reluctantly. 'As long as it isn't too much extra work for you.'

'Oh, I can cope,' Emma said with a smile. 'But what a disappointment for you. Still, maybe you won't care so much now you're dating Will; you'll be able to spend more time with him.'

There was that, of course, but Paris went back to her office feeling unhappy and frustrated. Not only were those three accounts the most prestigious that she had won, they were also the most lucrative, and as she was paid only a small basic salary and depended on bonuses to make up her money it meant a considerable drop in income.

If she had been able to go to the Brussels conference she might have generated some more work, but that too had gone to Emma, who, it seemed, had flown the company flag with some success. Paris tried not to be envious, but it was hard not to feel anger at a loss that was no fault of her own. That damn trial! But then she remembered that if it hadn't been for that she would never have met Will.

Her love affair, at least, was still going strongly. She and Will saw each other as often as possible and she often stayed overnight at his flat. The sex was just as good—better. He didn't seem as if he would ever have enough of her and delighted in her body, just as she gloried in giving him pleasure.

It wasn't only the sexual side of the relationship that was good; Will was terrific company and Paris loved just being with him. He had a great sense of the ridiculous, often making her laugh—sometimes even when she was trying to be serious. Life with Will was not only exciting but fun as well.

When they were apart her thoughts were full of him, and she would turn small things that happened to her into amusing anecdotes, anticipating with pleasure the way his eyes would fill with amusement as he laughed at them. Her feelings for him were growing ever deeper, far more so than anything she had ever experienced before, and she knew that she was in love.

Paris felt pretty confident that Will felt the same way about her, and she was staying with him so often that she thought he might ask her to move in with him. But they hadn't known each other very long yet so perhaps he felt it was too soon for that kind of commitment, because he didn't ask her.

Emma was still trying to be friendly with Will, even inviting him round to the flat to dinner, but Will still behaved distantly, maybe because Emma had coerced him into doing a few odd jobs around the place. She was pretty good at using people like that, putting on a 'helpless little woman' act to get people to do things for her, and would have used Paris the same way if Paris hadn't seen through the act and resisted, pointing out that they were supposed to share the chores.

A couple of months after the trial Paris went to a conference in Manchester for a few days. When she got back Emma regretfully told her that the rent on the flat had been increased quite substantially so she would, in turn, have to put Paris's share up, naming a much higher sum.

Paris looked at her with some dismay. 'But I can't possibly afford that much at the moment, Emma.' Worriedly, she pushed her hair back from her head. She had managed to find one new customer but the income no way made up for what she had lost.

'Well, I'm sorry, Paris. I wish I didn't have to ask you, but this is quite a luxurious flat, you know.'

'Yes, of course. I'll—I'll look round for somewhere else, then.'

'All right. I'll give you a month,' Emma offered.

Paris was taken aback; she hadn't expected to have to leave so soon, and for a moment felt a surge of resentment; it surely wouldn't have hurt Emma to let her take her time to find somewhere else? But Paris immediately felt ashamed; she had no idea of Emma's financial circumstances or what the total rent of the flat was. Maybe Emma had been subsidising her all this while, although she, Paris, had always paid her share of the rent promptly, as well as half the bills, which hadn't left a lot for herself.

That evening she developed a headache—a really bad one—and had to cancel her date with Will.

'You poor darling,' he said sympathetically. 'Would you like me to come round and stroke your brow?'

'Would that be all you would stroke?'

'Possibly not,' he admitted.

She chuckled but said, 'Maybe you'd better not, then.'

The headache got worse and, the following morning, was so bad that Emma had to drive them to work, and the elder girl advised her to see her doctor.

'Oh, no, I'm sure it will soon go,' Paris replied. 'I don't usually get headaches.'

'You're not pregnant, are you?' Emma asked, giving her a swift glance.

'No, definitely not.'

'OK. OK. I only asked.'

'Sorry, Emma,' Paris said contritely. 'But I am on the Pill; you know that.'

The headache went away eventually but a few days later she had another that was even worse. 'It sounds like a migraine to me,' someone told her, and so she went to the chemist and got some pills to try and relieve it, and they helped.

Out with Will one evening, he asked her to go to see a new film with him the following night, but she said, 'I'm sorry, I can't tomorrow.'

'Got another date?' he asked, raising his eyebrow. He was teasing; he was supremely confident that she wasn't interested in anyone else, as he had the right to be.

So he looked really surprised when she said, 'Sort of. I've arranged to go and look at a bedsit.'

His eyes settled on her face. 'Is Emma throwing you out?'

'No, but her rent has been put up and I can't afford my share any more, not after losing those three accounts. She's given me a month to find somewhere.'

'Generous of her,' Will commented wryly. He was silent for a moment, then said, 'Maybe it will be better if you do leave; I don't like you living with Emma.'

She always liked to think that her friends would get on well together and Paris felt a little disappointed. But the animosity seemed to be mutual because only recently Emma had commented rather acidly, 'Will may be incredible in bed, but his manners leave much to be desired. Still, if he suits you...' And she had given an eloquent shrug.

Paris had wanted to jump to Will's defence, but held her tongue; the two of them had taken a dislike to each other and that was that.

Looking at her now, Will gave a crooked smile—the one he used when he was teasing her. 'As a matter of fact I know of someone who's looking for a flatmate.'

Her heart skipped a beat, but she said, 'Really? Is it a nice flat?'

'Pretty good. All mod cons. Only, you might have to share a room.'

'I don't think I'd like that very much. How much is the rent?'

'Oh, I think you'd be able to afford the rent.'

'Well, I don't know. Who is this girl?'

'Girl?'

'The one who wants a flatmate.'

Leaning on his elbow, Will reached to take her hand, his grey eyes warm and mischievous. 'Who says it's a girl?'

Her eyes widened in mock innocence. 'You want me to share a room with some man?'

'Yes, please.'

She laughed, abandoning the demure look. 'When can I move in?'

'Would tomorrow do?'

Paris kissed the hand that held hers, her eyes alight with laughter and happiness. 'Tomorrow would be fine.' But then she felt compelled to add, 'So long as you're sure.'

'Of course I'm sure.'

'I wouldn't want you to feel pushed into it just because I can't afford to stay on with Emma.'

'Paris?'

'Yes?'

'Don't be silly.' And he leaned to kiss her on the mouth.

Moving in with Will was one of the most exciting times in Paris's life—having pretend arguments about wardrobe space, having him groan that he expected the bathroom to be festooned with drying underwear.

'I can dry it at the launderette,' she offered.

'Hell, no! I'm not going to have other men looking at that sexy black underwear of yours going round in the machine. I want to fantasise about it all by myself.'

She flung her arms round him, and kissed him exuberantly. 'God, I'm crazy about you, Will Brydon.'

'The feeling's mutual, ma'am.'

For the next couple of months everything was perfect, except that the wretched migraine attacks returned with painful frequency. But Paris was too happy to take much notice; she just pumped in headache pills until they went away.

She had to go to Europe a few times, once to a big convention in Prague where she was lucky enough to find two new accounts which put her more or less back on the income level she'd been on before. So she was able to insist on paying for all the food bills at the flat, although Will protested. But she felt happier paying her share.

She still saw Emma at work, of course, and they went out to lunch together on a regular basis, remaining friends but tacitly not discussing Will.

He and Paris were sharing their lives almost completely; Paris had taken him to meet each of her parents and their families, and both visits had been successful. In return Will took her to meet his elder brother, Mark, his only close relative since his parents had died some time ago. Mark, with his wife and two young children, lived in a village near Cambridge, where they invited Paris and Will to spend the weekend with them.

They set out from London around mid-morning; the day was fine and they were both in high spirits, Paris in particular looking forward to the trip. She wasn't at all nervous about meeting Will's relations; he'd told her a little about them, that they both had careers centred on Cambridge, and they sounded her kind of people.

The couple lived in an old, detached house, all stuccoed walls outside and beamed ceilings within, with an inglenook fireplace framed with a garland of dried hops. The walls of the downstairs sitting-room were rag-painted and then stencilled with an intricate flower design, as were all the cupboards in the traditional farm-house kitchen. The house looked like something out of a country-living-style magazine and Paris fell for the place at once.

Mark was seven years older than Will, and his wife, Annabel, looked to be about thirty. Their greeting was friendly enough, but both of them seemed a bit distracted. Mark, who was dressed in old jeans and a grease-stained T-shirt, gave them each a drink and said, 'You'll have to excuse me a minute; I was in the middle of cutting the grass when the damn mower broke down. Perhaps you could come and take a look at it, Will; you're better at mechanical things than I am.'

Will caught Paris's eye, gave a slight wink, and the two men went into the garden.

Annabel, dressed similarly to her husband, was kneeling before a four-oven Aga, almost in an attitude of worship, an anxious frown on her face as she looked at some cakes she was cooking. There seemed to be a lot of small cakes around, either cooling or waiting in trays to be cooked.

'Are you fond of cakes?' Paris asked curiously.

'What?' Annabel laughed and stood up. 'No, the village is having an open day tomorrow and I offered to make some cakes to sell with the teas. I think it's so important when you live in the country to take an active part in village life. Don't you?'

Paris had never thought about it, but it seemed that the question was merely rhetorical because Annabel glanced at her watch, gave an annoyed sigh, and said, 'Oh, Lord, I was supposed to pick up the girls from their dancing class ten minutes ago. And then I have to dash into town so that Olivia can buy a present for a friend's birthday. The party is this afternoon and she insists on choosing the present herself. Which is good, of course, don't you think? Children should have the right of choice. We were supposed to buy the present some time last week but somehow there was just too much happening.'

She knelt again at the Aga, took a batch of cakes out and put another lot in.

When she straightened, Paris knew what was coming but didn't volunteer. Annabel said, 'I know it's an awful cheek, but would you be an absolute angel and cook the rest of these cakes for me while I get the girls? I'm sorry to land it on you but it's one of those days.'

'I'm not very good at cooking and I've never used one of those cookers before,' Paris warned her.

'Oh, good heavens, you don't need any skill. Just have a look now and again to see if they're done. Thanks a million; I must fly.'

Annabel dashed upstairs, came down again ten minutes later wearing a smart town outfit, and ran outside to her car.

Those first few minutes seemed to set the tone for the whole weekend. Annabel rang on her personal phone about an hour later, full of apologies and asked Paris to start lunch for her. By the time she rushed in with her two daughters the lunch was ready and waiting; Will, having found out what was the matter with the mower and bought a new part from the local garden centre to fix it, was now mowing the large area of grass, and Mark was watering the plants in the greenhouse.

Paris thought that they'd relax over lunch but it seemed that the girls had to go to their violin lessons, arranged at an earlier time than usual because of the friend's birthday party, and they were already late.

'I'm sorry, I'll just have to rush,' Annabel said, and then, remembering, added, 'Oh, dear, I haven't shown you your room yet, have I? Never mind; Will knows where it is.'

It was a nice room, with views looking out on two sides over the garden and meadows beyond. But the bed hadn't yet been made up and they had to search for sheets and things and do it themselves. The walls were marked out for another stencil effect but were only partly done and there were no curtains on the windows.

'How long have they lived here?' Paris asked.

'About six years,' Will said laconically.

Paris was surprised; she'd have thought that Annabel would have finished the decorating by now.

When Annabel and her daughters hurried home an hour or so later, Olivia went up to have a bath and change into her party clothes and Charlotte, the younger child, immediately began to make a big fuss because she hadn't been invited.

'Never mind, darling. We'll do something really special together instead,' Annabel soothed.

'What? What will we do?' Charlotte naturally wanted to know.

'I'll think of something,' Annabel said, almost curtly, and she went to the stairs to yell at Olivia to hurry up. But when she took Olivia to the party, Annabel must have got sidetracked because she didn't come back, so it was left to Paris to try and amuse the younger child, but as Paris had no experience and Charlotte was grumpy it didn't work too well. Charlotte kept going to the window to look for her mother and when she didn't come went up to her room, locked herself in, and wouldn't come out or answer when Paris spoke to her.

Will, meanwhile was helping Mark to unblock some gutters; or, at least, Will was up the ladder doing so while Mark, who was supposed to be holding it, kept wandering off to dig his overgrown vegetable patch or to answer the phone, although most of the callers seemed to want Annabel.

That evening some friends had been invited to dinner, which Annabel cooked herself. She wasn't a bad cook, but, by the time she'd given the girls their pizzas, put them to bed, done the preparations for the meal, made half a dozen phone calls and got herself ready, it was very late before they sat down to eat, and almost three in the morning before the other guests left.

Curling tiredly up to Will, Paris said, 'Is it always like this?'

'Always,' he said resignedly.

The next day they were both roped in to help with the village open day, Paris helping Annabel in the tea tent and Will directing cars into the field being used as a car park, so they hardly saw one another. The main Sunday meal, to which Annabel liberally invited several neighbours, wasn't ready until eight in the evening, and Paris found herself doing most of the clearing up, as she had that morning because Annabel had been too tired to do it the night before.

It was midnight before they were able to drive back to London, Paris feeling more exhausted than she had when they'd arrived, and afraid that one of the blinding migraines was about to take over her head.

'Are you all right?' Will asked her when she grew silent. And when she admitted that her head ached he said angrily, 'I'm hardly surprised after the last two days. They don't have to live like that. They could well afford for Annabel not to work, but she insists on combining

the roles of wife, mother, career woman and active vil-
lager. And tries to be perfect at everything but with the
result that everything suffers.

'She's forever torn between her job, her home and her
family, and most of the time the job comes first. After
school and in the holidays the girls are looked after by
a child-minder or are farmed out to various friends. And
when Annabel *is* home she's always trying to decorate
the place in the latest fashion, or she's out at some village
organisation committee meeting.'

There was disgust in his voice as well as anger, but
Paris felt compelled to stand up for her sex and say, 'I'm
sure she's doing everything for the best.'

'That's just it; her intentions might be good but she
doesn't have the sense to see that she's achieving nothing.
Her family is suffering and so is she. She just cannot
manage that lifestyle.'

'What does Mark think about it?' Paris asked
guardedly.

Will shrugged. 'He's tried to persuade her to give up
her job but she won't. She says she won't be fulfilled if
she does.' The disgust was heavy again in his voice. 'If
she was so wrapped up in her career she shouldn't have
gone in for a family in the first place.'

'Rubbish!' Paris said shortly. 'A woman has every
right to have both a family and a career. Men do, don't
they? And thousands of women have children and *have*
to go out to work. Annabel isn't very organised, that's
all.'

Will gave a sarcastic snort. 'She tries to be all things
to all people and it doesn't work. You saw that for
yourself. And, the way I see it, bringing up children
should be a full-time job; they need all the help, edu-
cation and training they can to get to face
today's problems.

'There wouldn't be half the juvenile crime and adolescents with psychological problems if they'd got more attention at home. Most of them are thrust in front of the television screen to keep them quiet when they're babies and can work a video before they can talk. They become latchkey kids as soon as they go to school, and live off junk food for the rest of their lives.'

'Annabel cooks,' Paris protested.

'Yes, when she has a dinner party; the children don't often join in, and the rest of the week the girls live on stuff they take from the freezer and heat up in the microwave themselves. And there's virtually no consistency in their lives; they're often up till past midnight, are lucky if they have any clean and ironed clothes to wear, and are always rushing around to everything at the last minute. You saw them, Paris. There's no peace in that household; they never relax.

'And because Annabel insists on living in that big old house Mark spends every weekend doing repairs or working in the garden. And she's volunteered him for so many organisations that the poor chap is hardly at home during the week.'

'So maybe they should give up a few things,' Paris admitted, but added firmly, 'But she still has the right to work as well as have a family. Her career probably means a lot to her.'

'Nonsense. People shouldn't have children unless they are fully prepared to commit themselves to bringing them up properly. And anyway, her job is no big deal. She works in the computer department of a company that specialises in agricultural research, that's all. Hardly an indispensable position. Mark's job is far more important—and more lucrative.'

It might not seem much to a man, but Paris could well understand how much Annabel's job must mean to her. She'd probably trained and worked hard for it; she ought to be able to keep it if she wanted to. And although their life was hectic none of the family had appeared to be really unhappy. Mark seemed a little harassed, perhaps, but Annabel was warmly hospitable and they seemed to have loads of friends.

So Paris said stiffly, 'Why is it that men always think that women can't hold down a career and have children? Is it because men are so selfish or because they're afraid of the opposition, I wonder? Do they feel threatened by women and feel the need to do them down any way they can?'

Will threw her a surprised glance. 'Don't tell me you're a feminist.'

'And why not?' Paris retorted. 'You're obviously dead against married women having a career.'

'I'm against mothers working when they don't have to,' he returned shortly. 'Especially Annabel. She just can't cope, and there's going to be some sort of crisis in that household before long. It's inevitable. Charlotte has already had to see a child counsellor. I ask you—a kid of seven!'

'You can't blame that on Annabel. Charlotte is probably highly strung or something.'

'Rubbish!' Will exclaimed. 'She needs a full-time mother. It's Annabel who is completely selfish. If she wanted a career then she shouldn't have had children in the first place. I blame Mark; he ought to put his foot down and insist that Annabel stay at home. I told him so, too.'

Paris gave a gasp of consternation. 'How can you possibly be so bigoted? What happens when the children leave school and go out to work themselves? Annabel will be really stuck at home then. She'll have lost years out of her career and will be lucky if she gets another job.'

'So she could do voluntary typing for a charity or something, if she feels the need,' Will said shortly.

'Voluntary work!' Paris said in appalled disgust. 'That would really be a challenge, wouldn't it? How very fulfilling. Something easy and unstressful for the little woman to do in the odd moments when she isn't waiting hand and foot on her husband!'

Hearing the sarcasm in her tone, Will said curtly, 'This is a futile argument, and purely hypothetical anyway, because I doubt if Annabel will ever be persuaded to give it up.'

'Then good for her,' Paris said vehemently. 'If Mark has any sense he should encourage her, not—' A piercing pain shot through her head and she broke off, suddenly realising that they were doing more than just arguing. Biting her lip, she leaned back in her seat and closed her eyes tightly.

'A migraine?' Will asked, glancing at her.

She nodded silently, wincing as she did so.

'You're getting too many of them. You must go and see your doctor first thing tomorrow.'

'It will go; there's nothing to make a fuss about.'

'Aren't I allowed to worry about you, then? Is advising you to see your doctor interfering in *your* career?' Will said on an acerbic note.

For a moment they were both silent, both shocked that they were quarrelling, then burst out together:

'I'm sorry; I didn't mean that.'

'I want you to worry about me; of course I do.'

Will gave a rueful sigh and put his hand over Paris's. 'It's been a dreadful weekend, hasn't it?'

'Exhausting,' she admitted.

'Please, darling, go and see your doctor about these headaches.'

'All right, I promise.'

* * * *

Paris went, and when she found out the probable cause wished she'd gone earlier, because her doctor said, 'It's more than likely that the contraceptive pill you're taking doesn't agree with you. I'll put you on a different one and see if it helps. Finish off your current month's pills, though.'

Paris didn't see much point in doing that if it was the darn pills that were giving her the migraines, so left them off at once and started on the new ones. She felt a bit odd and unwell for a couple of weeks but the symptoms finally settled down and then she felt fine and the headaches seemed to clear like magic.

It was because of the change over from one lot of pills to another that at first she took no notice when her period failed to arrive. But when nothing happened the following month she began to get worried and could no longer dismiss it.

Emma, at lunch one day, noticed her preoccupation and asked her straight out what was the matter. Paris hesitated, then told her. 'It can't be anything disastrous, of course,' she added, confidence in her voice. 'I've been on either one pill or the other the whole time.'

'Well, you'd better make sure,' Emma said practically. 'Buy one of those do-it-yourself pregnancy test kits.'

Paris laughed. 'I'll be wasting my money.' But a few days later, when still nothing happened, she bought one anyway—and was stunned when it showed up positive. Sure that there must have been a mistake, she tried the second test in the kit, and nearly died when she got the same result. A visit to her doctor confirmed the catastrophic fact that she was pregnant.

Will was away at the time; he had gone with some friends to the South of France, to sail a yacht that one of them had bought back in England.

'Trust a man to be away and out of contact when you most need him,' Paris said to Emma rather shakily.

They were round at Emma's flat, Paris having gone round there in a highly emotional state, badly needing to talk to someone. Emma was alone, not yet having found anyone to take Paris's place, even though it had been several months since she'd moved out.

Emma looked at her for a moment, then said deliberately, 'Maybe it's just as well. You'll be able to think about it logically. Things tend to get uptight when men are around.'

'I hope Will will be pleased,' Paris said nervously. 'I'm not at all sure how he feels about children.'

Emma gave a laugh of astonishment. 'You're surely not going to tell him about this?'

Paris frowned. 'But I'll have to tell him.'

'Why? What has it got to do with him?'

'Emma! It has everything to do with Will, surely?'

'Did he ask you to get pregnant?'

'No, of course not. But—'

'Then why tell him? Did *you* intend to?'

'No, but—'

'Then I hope that you're not going to let a slip like this ruin your whole life.'

Paris stared at her. 'What are you talking about?'

'Why, a termination, of course. You surely aren't even considering keeping it?'

'Well, yes. It's a baby,' Paris said in consternation.

'Rubbish. It's just a fertilised egg, that's all. Something that has happened by accident, at entirely the wrong time in your life. And in Will's. And it's up to you to be sensible and put things right, not get all sentimental and mawkish.'

'I'm not. But it would be wrong to—'

'Do you want to ruin Will's life?' Emma cut in bluntly.

Paris looked at her in dismay. 'No, of course not. But would it really be so terrible? I—I haven't really had time to think it through yet.'

'Of course it would. You'd have to give up your job for a start.'

'Not necessarily. I could hire—'

'Of course you would,' Emma interrupted vehemently. 'I've seen other girls in your position who've tried to go it alone. It never works. The company took you on because you're a free agent, didn't they? So how can you go flying off all over Europe and, in time, all over the world when you're saddled with a baby?'

'It wouldn't be just me,' Paris protested. 'It would be Will's baby too, and he would help take care of it.' But even as she said the words Paris had a vivid memory of their quarrel about working mothers after that disastrous visit to Will's brother, and her voice trailed off.

Emma burst into laughter. 'Oh, Paris, you innocent. Haven't you learned anything about men? Everything is lovely with Will now; of course it is. He has a mistress who looks after him like a wife *and* who pays her way. What more could a man ask for, for heaven's sake?

'But if a baby came along all that would change. He'd be expected to stay home and do chores, to provide for you both, and to watch you become more interested in the child than in him. And you'd lose your figure and always be too tired to be any good at sex any more.'

'You don't paint a very pleasant picture,' Paris said shakily.

'But a true one, I assure you.'

'What about married couples? They have children. If they didn't the world would come to an end.'

'When a man asks a woman to marry him, it means he's ready to settle down, to take on that commitment.' Emma saw Paris's head go down and made a shrewd guess. 'And Will hasn't asked you to marry him, has he?'

Paris shrugged, shook her head. 'We haven't known each other long enough for that yet.'

'But if you have this baby you'll be forcing him to make that commitment—whether he likes it or not. Do you really want to force him into that?'

Frowning, Paris shook her head. 'No, but he has a right to know so that we can discuss the—the choices together.'

'Rubbish! If you do that, you're giving him no choice at all. He'll think you're putting the onus on him, making him take the decision. The responsibility, then, will be his.

'Think about it; if he says to keep the baby he will have to support you both for the rest of your life. And if he says have an abortion then he'll always feel guilty—and you'll always blame him for it. Every time you row you'll throw it in his face until he can't take it any more and walks out.'

Paris's face had paled, but she said, 'But what if Will says keep it and we get married?'

Emma laughed rather scornfully. 'Then, again, every time you have a row he'll blame you for trapping him, and it will go on forever more—or until he decides to go and look for the freedom he lost and walks out on you anyway.'

Appalled at the prospect, Paris said faintly, 'A no-win situation.'

'I'm afraid so, my dear.'

Feeling as if she was fighting a battle, Paris said, 'But lots of people have been caught this way in the past and have survived, have had happy marriages.'

'Oh, yes, in the past, but not so much nowadays. And especially when the girl wants to keep her career, as I'm sure you do. Perhaps if you were willing to give up everything and just become Will's wife, the baby's mother...' Emma shrugged. 'If you'd be satisfied with that, then maybe it might work out.'

Paris stared at her, remembering how scathing Will had been about Annabel keeping on with her career. He'd said quite definitely then that people shouldn't have children unless they were willing to commit themselves entirely to their upbringing. She felt a chill settle on her heart; she wasn't ready to give everything up. Not yet. Not so soon. But if it meant keeping the baby...

Emma was saying, 'Really, Paris, I think you'd be acting in Will's best interests if you didn't tell him. Unless you make up your mind to keep the baby, of course. But I really can't see any reason to do so. It was just a mistake. Anyone must realise that. I mean, you were behaving very responsibly, and it wasn't your fault that this happened.'

Paris thought guiltily about how she hadn't followed her doctor's instructions to the letter, but said desperately, 'I *have* to keep it. I have to go through with it.'

Emma shrugged. 'Of course. If you've made up your mind to as good as finish your life now. But don't expect Will to stand by you.'

'But he will. You don't know him!' Paris said almost on a sob.

Coming to put her arms round her, Emma said with a sigh, 'I'm sorry, Paris, but it's a fact of life. There are some men who just don't want children, and I'm very much afraid Will is one of them. As soon as he finds out, things will change completely between you. He'll either leave, or if he stays it will be out of a sense of duty. Is that really what you want?'

Paris shook her head wordlessly, horrified more by the latter prospect than by anything else.

'It would be a great shame to spoil both your lives because of a silly little thing like this. Now wouldn't it?'

Emma went on persuasively. 'It would be quite devastating for Will, I know. It always is for a man. And, as you said, you haven't known each other long enough yet. So why rush into making the biggest mistake of your life? You want to go on learning about each other, taking your time, letting your love develop. And this silly mistake could be all put right so easily and with so little fuss. It's so commonplace now. Will—no one—need ever know. I know a clinic where you could go. And I'd come with you if you liked, to hold your hand, make sure you're OK.'

Paris was very pale, her hands balled into tight fists. 'But what about the—the baby?' She found it very hard to say the word.

Emma stood and put her hands on her shoulders. 'You mustn't worry about that. It's nothing yet. Nothing at all. But, I beg of you, Paris, if you want to go on with Will as you were, then get this mistake, *which is no fault of yours*, out of the way, and get on with your lives. Will would want that, I'm sure. You *must* do it, for his sake. You do see that, don't you? Don't you?' she said more forcefully when Paris didn't answer.

Slowly, reluctantly, Paris nodded.

'That's very sensible of you. And I know Will would love you even more for it.' She smiled at Paris. 'Sometimes we women have to be very strong for the sake of the men we love, you know.'

The next few days were the worst that Paris had ever known. She was constantly torn first one way and then the other, couldn't sleep, couldn't eat, and definitely couldn't concentrate at work, especially with Emma there continuously pushing her to have a termination quickly.

Pleading illness, Paris stayed at home, hoping for quiet, but Emma was immediately on the phone, telling her to make up her mind, not to leave it a day longer, and she even came round in the evening, pushing, all the time pushing her to have the operation. And always emphasising that, one way or another, she would lose Will if she didn't.

He was still away, and Paris alternately longed for his return and was afraid that he might come back before she'd had the abortion. *If* she had it.

Paris pressed her hands against her head in distress, not knowing what to do. If only Will wasn't so fiercely anti working mothers; then she wouldn't have had any hesitation in keeping the baby. But she would be miserable if she didn't work, she just knew it. She needed the challenge of looking for new markets, needed the highs of success—what else had she been training for all these years, for heaven's sake? She was too young to give everything up, and a future of just staying at home for the next twenty years looked bleak indeed.

After another stress-filled night of gazing sleeplessly into the darkness, Paris felt really ill and half-crazy with indecision. She dragged herself out of bed, still not finally decided but coming closer to contemplating having the termination.

It went against her conscience, against her beliefs, but she felt that she must do it for Will's sake, not for her own. Her mind was filled with a terrible dread of forcing him into a marriage that he didn't want, of seeing their happiness fade into misery, and love into hate. If he loved her.

Paris knew that she loved him utterly, but he had never come right out and said that he loved her, although she had been sure that he did—before this, before Emma's arguments had completely undermined her confidence. She convinced herself that her first concern must be for Will, to protect him from her terrible mistake, but even as the thought filled her mind she had to stifle not only her own guilt but also the knowledge that she would do anything not to lose him.

That morning she phoned Emma and said painfully, 'I—I'm thinking of going to the clinic today. Will you come with me?'

But the older girl was busy and unable to make it. 'I'm dreadfully sorry, but I'm taking a training course this morning, and this afternoon there's a meeting I just have to go to,' Emma said with concern. 'Can't you go another time? But no, better not. You really should have it done as soon as possible.'

'Yes. Don't worry. I'll—I'll go alone.'

'Isn't there anyone else who—?'

'No. Goodbye, Emma.' Paris put the phone down and bit her knuckles hard, fighting back tears. She had said that she would go alone but she wasn't at all sure that she had the courage, or that she was indeed going to go through with it. If ever she had needed a friend it was now. Unable to stay in the flat, Paris put on her coat and went out for a long walk in the park, striding along, trying desperately to make up her mind.

She came upon a group of young women pushing their small children along in modern Baby Buggies. The women didn't look particularly well dressed but they all looked happy, content. And the babies looked so sweet.

Paris hadn't taken much notice of babies before, but as she came to the group, which had stopped to feed the ducks on the pond, she slowed and looked at them. One in particular caught her eye—a boy, she was sure, with such soft skin, a pretty little nose and great blue eyes that looked up at her so trustingly. Suddenly he gave her a toothless smile and Paris knew then that there was only one course open to her, that there had never really been a choice at all.

Quickly, smiling to herself with relief, she turned and strode towards the park entrance and home. She was going to phone Will, tell him without another moment's delay.

There were several teenage boys in the park riding their mountain bikes, racing each other, swerving round the trees and bushes. As she hurriedly rounded a bend in the path, almost running in her eagerness, she found one boy coming straight at her.

Paris gave a cry of warning and the boy swerved. But Paris had jumped to avoid him and had gone the same way. He cannoned into her and she lost her footing, falling down a steep grassy bank, rolling over and over until she came to a stop with a thud, face-on to a tree. The boy, frightened, cycled away fast.

Two women walking their dogs came to help her up, brushing at her coat, saying that the cyclists were a menace, asking if she was hurt. Paris didn't feel hurt—her coat had saved her as she'd rolled—but she'd hit the tree hard across her waist and hips.

The accident had shaken her, so she stood for a few minutes, leaning against the tree, until she felt recovered enough to leave the women and walk on. But as soon as she left the park Paris took a taxi home, and laid down on the bed to rest. It was less than an hour later that she started to bleed, and the choice that she'd so agonised over was no longer hers.

When Emma phoned the next day Paris was still in bed, feeling weak.

'How are you? Have you had it done?'

The questions brought back all the torments of the last few days and Paris's voice was heavy with distress as she said, 'It's gone. The baby's gone.'

'Was it very bad? Would you like me to come over?'

'No! Just leave me alone. And I don't want to talk about it, Emma. Do you understand? Never, ever mention it again.' And she put down the phone, cutting the other girl off.

Will came home a few days later, but she told him nothing of what she'd been through. He was so happy, so pleased to be home that there was no way she was going to spoil it.

A week after the miscarriage she felt physically much the same as ever. Mentally—it was different. Paris tried to put it out of her mind, but that was very difficult. She was consumed by guilt, sure that if she hadn't contemplated a termination she would never have lost the baby. OK, it was the fall that had actually caused it, but if she hadn't been so stressed out, felt so wretched, she wouldn't have been in the park in the first place. Paris blamed herself; she should have followed her conscience, not listened to Emma.

Even the inner knowledge that there was now no fear of losing Will gave her no comfort. Emma, seeing her dejection, advised her to forget the whole thing and received an angry flash from Paris's green eyes that made her hastily drop the subject.

At home with Will it was easier; he was so full of his holiday with his friends, so eager for her that she soon began to feel happier. Sometimes, though, she was a little withdrawn, but when Will asked her what was the matter she just shrugged it off and tried to be again the laughing, uncomplicated girl he wanted.

It was a few weeks later when Paris became aware that people at work were talking about her. When she walked into the ladies' room one day there were some girls there who immediately stopped talking when she came in and gave her strangely shocked looks. It was the same look that she had noticed on a couple of other people's faces recently but had ignored. She found, too, that some of the older members of the staff were no longer so friendly, while one or two of the men, conversely, became much too friendly.

One of them, with a reputation as a womaniser, came into her office when she was alone and shut the door. Paris was standing at a filing cabinet and turned, giving her usual bright smile until she saw who it was. 'What can I do for you?' she asked coolly.

'Ah, what couldn't you do for me? How about coming out for a drink with me tonight for a start?'

'No, thanks.'

'Why not? You might enjoy it.' And the man put his hand on her hip.

Paris swung round furiously, knocking his hand away. 'How dare you touch me? Get out of here, or I'll report you for sexual harassment.'

He laughed in her face. 'Who's going to believe you— with your reputation? Besides, it wouldn't look good on your record, would it? And we all know you'd do anything to keep your job, to further your career.'

'What are you talking about?' she demanded angrily.

'As if you didn't know,' he jeered. 'But you wouldn't have to worry if you were with me; I'd make sure you didn't get pregnant and have to get rid of it.'

She stared at him, for a moment too shocked to speak. But then she felt a surge of the most terrible anger that she had ever felt in her life, far too forceful for her to bother to deny his accusation. Filled by it, too over-whelmed to stop and think, she bit out, 'A wimp like you wouldn't have the balls to make anyone pregnant!' Then she strode to the door and jerked it open. 'Now get out of here, you creep.'

If looks could have killed she would have been an-nihilated. 'You'll pay for that, you slut,' he gritted. But at least he walked away.

Paris sat down at her desk and put her head in her hands. So that was what was wrong: they all thought she'd had an abortion. And there was only one way they could have found out. From Emma. Emma, who was supposed to be her friend.

But had she been such a friend? Paris remembered the way the older girl had taken over her special accounts and kept them for her own. Was that from jealousy, because Paris had started to get really successful and show that she had a bright future in the company? Had Emma been afraid for her own job? And then there was the way she had kicked Paris out of the flat. That too had been more the action of an enemy than a friend. And now this.

Paris sat there for some time, and in that time lost a lot of her trusting nature. She supposed that she could go round the office and tell them all the truth. But would they believe her? To hell with them all, she thought suddenly. I don't give a damn what they think. So long as I have Will then nothing else matters. She came out of her office with her head high, and it stayed that way.

But she knew that she would have to tell Will that night—tell him everything. But she was held up in the traffic getting home, then had to rush to change because they were going out to dinner with another couple, so there wasn't a chance. And the next morning she was jetting off early to Milan for another conference, so she reluctantly decided to leave it until she got back. This sort of confession would need more time; they would need to talk it through.

While she was away, Paris rang Will every day as she always did. The first couple of days were fine; he was as warm towards her as always, telling her about his day and how much he missed her. But the third time she called, and the day after that, all she got was her own voice on the answering machine. It could have been that she'd missed him, of course, but Paris had a sense of foreboding and couldn't wait to fly home.

He didn't meet her at the airport and the minute she walked into the flat she knew that her world was in ruins. Her cases, all her things, were standing piled in the hall. Will was sitting in the armchair in the lounge, waiting for her. He didn't get to his feet. His face was granite, his eyes like the coldest sea, as he said, his voice as cutting as a razor blade, 'Had another abortion while you were away?'

She flinched as if he really had cut her, and went very pale. 'No! I suppose Emma told you,' she said bitterly.

'Emma? I might have known she'd have something to do with it. No, I found out that you'd destroyed my child from some filthy swine from your office who sought me out in a pub. He knew it all,' Will said with tormented bitterness. 'And he knew that I didn't know a thing about it. He laughed in my face as he told me, enjoyed doing it.'

'I hope you knocked his head off,' Paris said in helpless rage. He didn't answer and she took a step towards him, her hands reaching out to him like a supplicant's. 'I didn't have an abortion. I—'

'Are you saying that you weren't pregnant?'

'No, but—'

'And are you pregnant now?'

'No,' she admitted wretchedly. 'But you don't—'

'No, I know you're not—none better.' His voice suddenly rose as he lost control of his anger. 'How could you? How could you even contemplate having an abortion? And don't insult me by saying you didn't.'

Guilt made her admit defensively, 'Well, yes, in a way. But only because of you. I thought you'd want me to and—'

'How *dare* you?' Will shouted the words at her, leaping to his feet, his face filled with ungovernable rage. 'How dare you say that you did it for my sake? How dare you presume to know what I want? If you think I'm the kind of man who would encourage—or even *allow* you to do something like this then you know nothing about me. Nothing!'

The last word came out explosively, his face rigid with rage and disgust, his hands balled into white-knuckled fists. Paris stared at him in appalled dismay, too stunned by his anger to defend herself, to try and explain.

Striding towards her, Will caught hold of her and pro-pelled her towards the door. 'Get out of here! Get out of my life!'

'Will, no! Please.' She tried to cling to him, but he dragged her towards the door and pushed her outside it.

She was crying now but he took no notice, just picked up her things and dumped them down in the corridor beside her. She grabbed his arm and hung on to it des-perately, as if by holding him she could make him understand, make him realise how much she needed him. But he shook her off, pushed her roughly against the wall, then went back into the flat and slammed the door shut behind him.

Paris tried hammering on the door and calling through the letter box but he took no notice, and he had bolted the door so she couldn't get in. She sat on the floor outside, sobbing uncontrollably, repeating his name over and over like a prayer.

The front door of the building opened and a taxi driver came in. He came up the stairs, hesitated when he saw her, checked the number of the flat and looked at her uncomfortably before saying, 'I've been told to come and take you to a hotel, miss.'

It was then that Paris knew that it was over. If Will was this determined to be rid of her then it was finished. She gave up then, painfully, achingly aware that by not telling him everything she had lost him for ever.

Somehow she dragged herself to her feet and, her breath still coming in heartbroken sobs, helped the driver carry her things to the taxi. Outside on the pavement she turned and looked up at the window of the flat. Will was there, watching. But he immediately turned away and she was left, her heart desolated, to get into the cab and let it drive her away.

CHAPTER THREE

Now the train thundered on through the night, a harsh background to the tormented memories that filled Paris's mind. The inspector had said that she would be able to shut herself away, but there was no comfort in that; it was inevitable that she and Will would cross paths however much she tried to avoid him—and he her, of course. And for the life of her Paris didn't know how to play it, what to do, what to say if they came face to face.

She sighed and tried to put it out of her mind, dozed a little, only to wake with a start of fear as she remembered the ordeal that lay ahead of her. It was before dawn when they got out of the train at a small, deserted station. Another car, or rather a van, was waiting. Paris had to climb in the windowless back and it was almost half an hour later that she was helped out, feeling cold and cramped.

She was standing in the open courtyard of a very large stone building that looked much too big to be just a house. The stone was weather-beaten and looked old, as did the very high wall that surrounded the courtyard. For an astonished moment Paris thought that they'd brought her to a prison, but then she saw a discreet notice near the double wooden doors of the building: 'The Castle Hotel'. Some hotel!

Lifting her eyes, she took in the turreted towers at each corner, the heavy shutters that could be drawn across the windows on its four floors. The air felt much colder than in London and when she looked round Paris could make out the snow-capped peaks of some distant hills just showing over the wall. Some instinct told her that she was in Scotland, and that it must have been quite far north for such a long journey.

'Let's go in,' the policewoman said, catching her arm.

The driver followed with her cases and they went into the castle-cum-hotel, the door opened for them by a burly-looking man in jeans and a loose knitted sweater. He obviously knew her escort because he nodded and stood aside to let them in. 'The last one?' he asked.

'Yes, that's the lot. They're all yours,' the driver said.

The man turned to Paris, who was feeling resentful at being treated like a parcel. 'I'm Captain Waters,' he told her. 'Mike Waters.'

'Captain?' Paris didn't think they had that rank in the police force.

'Army,' he explained. 'We're helping out. First I must tell you the rules. You must not, in any way, try to communicate with anyone outside. Not by phone, letter or any other means. Do you understand?'

'Yes, of course.'

The captain gave her an assessing look, then nodded. 'OK. I'll take you up to your room and then I'll show you round the place.'

'Are you in charge?'

He nodded. 'Together with a chief inspector in the police.'

Her room was on the third floor at the back of the building, looking out over a huge expanse of forest— but the serrated ranks of a man-made forest of fir trees, not the natural variety. They shouldn't have much difficulty in getting a Christmas tree, Paris thought cynically as she unpacked yet again.

Luckily the clothes she'd taken on her European trip had been mainly her smart business wear, so she'd had enough left in her wardrobe to bring clean things with her. But they were mostly casual clothes—jeans and sweaters, together with a few dresses. A rueful smile came to her lips as she hung them up; unfortunately the monthly fashion glossies didn't give any advice on what one should pack for an indefinite period under police protection.

When she went down into the entrance hall Mike Waters was waiting for her. He took her round the ground floor, into the galleried dining-room containing a dozen round tables, where a couple of waiters were setting places for breakfast.

'The staff here...?' she questioned.

'The place is always closed in the winter so most of the staff have gone home. Those that have stayed all live in. They have worked here for years and have been completely vetted. Some of our own men have taken the places of those that have gone.'

'There seem to be an awful lot of people here,' she said, counting the place settings and multiplying by the number of tables.

'Several people have had to bring their family with them; they couldn't say they were going away for Christmas and leave their family behind, could they?'

Paris hadn't thought of that. It gave her some comfort to think that she could probably hide among so many.

Captain Waters took her on to see the television-room, the bar—a room tarted up with too much tartan—the lounge, the ballroom, the card-room, and told her that there was a pool and a gymnasium in the basement. There seemed to be no end to the place. Again she was thankful; if she saw Will coming she would easily be able to slip away somewhere else. Maybe this situation wouldn't be as bad as she'd feared.

It was, though. It was far worse than she could have imagined.

It wasn't yet seven o'clock—too soon for all the 'guests' to come down—but because of her long journey Paris was offered an early breakfast. She accepted with alacrity, not only because she was hungry, but so that she could eat and be out of the room before Will came down.

She helped herself to orange juice and a cheerful waiter brought her a plate of scrambled eggs on toast and a pot of steaming coffee. Paris sat down at a table near the window to eat, thinking that she'd never had a meal in such circumstances before.

At the far end of the room a door opened but she took no notice and didn't glance in that direction, thinking that it was one of the waiters. But then some instinct, some primitive awareness, made her look up.

Will was standing just inside the door, staring across the room at her. It was a very large room and they were at opposite ends of it, but she could see the tension in his body and face, the grim hardness of his jaw, the coldness in his eyes. For a long—eternally long—moment they stared at each other, the atmosphere becoming taut, electric. But then Will abruptly turned, pulled out a chair at a nearby table, and sat down in it, his back very deliberately turned towards her.

Paris looked blindly down at her plate and went to eat but found that her hands were shaking. Damn! Damn!

But why damn fate? she thought bitterly. She ought to be used to the tricks it was continually playing on her by now. Reaching out, she managed to pick up the cup of coffee and took a drink. It was hot—too hot, really— but it made her feel a degree better.

So Will was going to ignore her. That was the way he wanted to play it. Well, OK, that would probably make life easier, physically. But it would do nothing to relieve this terrible tension that still filled the room even though they were no longer staring at each other. It was like a tangible thing, so strong that when the waiter came in Paris expected him to have to fight his way through it, and was amazed when he just got calmly on with his work and then went out again.

Will was wearing a tracksuit and she guessed that he must have been either working out in the gym or jogging. Not that he'd jogged early in the day when they'd been living together, but then they'd had far more interesting things to do in the mornings. Biting her lip, Paris pushed that thought away, afraid that Will might read her mind.

She tried to eat her eggs and could only pick at them, her hunger gone, but pride demanded that she didn't just get up and walk away. She must sit it out, not let him think that seeing him had made her a trembling wreck.

Thankfully, a few more early risers came in—some adults and several young children. They greeted Will and looked at Paris with open curiosity. Under cover of the noise they made Paris was able hurriedly to finish her breakfast and leave, her going hopefully hidden by the arrival of more people.

She kept her face averted so didn't know whether Will saw her go, but then realised from her own relief at being out of the room that, if nothing else, he would probably be aware of the lack of tension. Not bothering to wait for the lift, she ran up the wide staircase to her room and threw herself down in the armchair. She should never have let the police persuade her into coming here. Any danger would have been better than this.

It was impossible not to think of Will. He was alone, so did that mean that he wasn't married? But maybe he was and it was just that his wife didn't jog. Or maybe they'd made love last night and she was too tired.

Fighting a fierce surge of jealousy towards this unknown woman, Paris gripped the arms of the chair in torment. The frustration after Will had left her had been dreadful; she had longed for him with a deep ache that time had done little to assuage. It had been almost as bad as the pain that filled her heart and the guilt that was a constant torment.

No matter that she hadn't actually had a termination; she had been persuaded to think of it—think seriously. For the millionth time she wished that she'd acted on her own instincts and never listened to Emma's poison. But she'd been so young and unsure of herself, so gullible. And finding herself pregnant had so shocked her that her emotions had been all over the place. But if only—

Paris realised what she was doing and forcibly turned her mind from the subject. She had taught herself not to dwell on the past, to turn her mind to other things. She had succeeded to a large extent, but that had been when Will had no longer been there. Now, after seeing him this morning, it was almost impossible.

Paris had been determined not to skulk away but to face up to her loss and to try and find new interests to take her mind off it. Those new interests also included new men, but there had been no one else, although Paris had had offers enough.

Sometimes it angered her that men found her so attractive; she gave them no encouragement, was open in her lack of interest, but had come to wonder if it wasn't that very lack that drew men to her. Perhaps they were piqued by her indifference, felt that to win her over would be a challenge. Or perhaps they were drawn by the air of mystery that her coolness created.

Either way, they were doomed to disappointment. However nice, however good-looking they were themselves, whatever they did to try to attract her, they withered away when they were unable to light a flame in her cool green eyes. Paris watched them go without regret; why settle for the commonplace when you had known the best?

There was the sound of laughter outside. Going to the window, Paris opened it and looked out. Some children were playing in the courtyard. Well wrapped-up against the cold, they were playing a chasing game, their shrieks of excitement echoing back from the stone walls.

Paris watched them, wondering what her and Will's child would have been like. Would he have had Will's dark hair or have been red-headed like herself? It was always like this: whenever she saw a child she would start to wonder, to imagine. And in her imagination the child was always a boy. In her dreams too—those recurring dreams in which she and Will were still together, married, in their own house with a garden, and so wonderfully happy with their son. Then Paris would slowly, reluctantly awaken, to realise again what she had lost, and face again the eternal loneliness that was to be her punishment. With a sigh, she pulled the window shut and made herself go downstairs again.

A well-rounded middle-aged woman was walking through the hall from the dining-room as she came down the staircase. 'Hello.' The woman stopped. 'You must be the last member of our party. We were starting to get worried about you.' The woman spoke as if this were just an ordinary house party, as if being worried meant being concerned that Paris might not turn up, certainly not fearing that she might have been injured or even murdered.

'I've been away,' Paris explained. 'I only got back yesterday.'

'Well, I'm glad you got here safely.' The woman held out her hand. 'I'm Gwenda Paston, the judge's wife.'

Mrs Paston took Paris under her wing, taking her into the big lounge and introducing her to many people she didn't know and recalling several members of the jury to her memory. Paris sat down with a woman juror who was there with her husband—both broad Londoners—and soon the woman was gossiping away at full tilt.

It seemed that most of the people involved in the case had already been at the Castle Hotel for nearly ten days and had got to know one another. Amusements had been thought up to while away the time: bridge tournaments, talks on a whole variety of subjects and professions, craft lessons—making Christmas cards had been a very popular one, Paris was told.

'But surely you couldn't send them from here, could you?' she asked.

'No, they were all taken down to London and sent from there.'

Everyone seemed to be very blasé about their loss of liberty and the threat imposed by Noel Ramsay to their lives, but then they'd already had time to get used to it and to feel safe amongst so many others. They'd had more time, too, to prepare themselves to come here and had brought their hobbies and other projects to work on: several women were doing some kind of needlework, a man sat in a corner patiently cataloguing his stamp collection, another was doing marquetry.

But mostly people sat around and chatted, enjoying getting to know one another better, which Paris found to be an advantage when she so casually said, 'Are all the jury members here with their wives and husbands?'

'Most of us, although there are one or two single people. One man is divorced now, and then there's Will Brydon—he's alone. You must remember him—didn't you used to have your lunch together when the trial was on?'

'Why, yes, I think I do remember,' Paris said, and added offhandedly, 'He's still single, is he?'

'It seems so, although he's got quite friendly with one of the witnesses this last week. One of the girls Ramsay used to go with.' The woman chuckled. 'Although I doubt whether Will Brydon will go on being so friendly when he sees that you've arrived.'

It was meant as a compliment, Paris knew, and she smiled her thanks as she wondered just how 'friendly' Will had become with the other girl. It was to her own advantage, of course: it would keep him busy, make it less likely for them to bump into each other. But even though she told herself this very firmly Paris couldn't avoid the stab of pain that pierced her heart.

'How about you, dearie?' the woman asked. 'Are you still single?'

'Oh, yes.' Paris smiled, but suddenly saw a way that she could protect herself a little. 'Although I do have a close friend,' she added impulsively, banking on the woman being such a gossip that this titbit of information would soon go the rounds and reach Will's ears.

They were joined by some other people and Paris made sure that she stayed with them through lunch, and afterwards went with them to watch a video film in the television-room. Later, however, the group broke up, most of them going up to their rooms to prepare for dinner, which Paris was told was served early, at seven o'clock.

There was a small crowd of people waiting for the lifts so Paris opted for the stairs. She was crossing the landing to go up the second flight when she met Will coming down the opposite way.

She kept her head down, was ready to walk past without looking at him, but he slowed, then said, his voice reluctant, 'Paris?'

Her hand gripping the wide banister rail tightly, she raised her eyes to look at him. At first she thought he looked no different, but then she saw that the three years had changed him. His cheeks were thinner, and his left eyebrow—the one that had had the humorous quirk—

now seemed to have a cynical lift to it. His mouth, too, had a little twist at the corner, making him look as if he regarded the world with some derision, found it wanting. But his thick dark hair was the same, and she recognised the coldness in his eyes, even though she had only ever seen it there twice before: this morning—and on the night he had thrown her out of his life.

'Hello, Will.' She tried to speak calmly, to let no emotion show, but the words came out on an unsteady breath.

'Strange circumstances to meet in,' he commented. He was looking her over, taking in her tall, slim figure, her shoulder-length red hair, and the attractiveness of her face, dominated by her green eyes. Once there would have been admiration in his gaze; now his features were a stony mask.

'Yes, aren't they?'

There was a pause which grew heavy. Paris went to move on, but then Will said, 'Why did you take so long to get here?'

'I was away. Working.'

'Ah, yes, your precious job,' he said on a sardonic note. 'I suppose you're still with that company?'

'Yes, I still work for them,' she answered. There was a story to that—one that concerned him in a way, she supposed—but Paris wasn't about to tell him.

Will gave a mocking grin. 'And I suppose you're their blue-eyed girl, the leading light of the sales department by now?'

'I have my own team and my own area, yes,' she admitted, her chin coming up a little at his tone.

'Somehow I just knew you would have.' The contempt in his voice was more open now. 'After all, it always was the most important thing in your life, wasn't it?'

Will's face had hardened and his eyes were narrowed in scarcely suppressed scorn. After seeing him at breakfast Paris knew that there was still tension between them, but it still came as a shock to see how deeply he still cared about what had happened.

Picking her words, she said, 'It is *now*, yes.'

By saying it that way she wanted to let him know that he had once been the most important thing in her life, that there had been nothing but work since they had split up. A stupid thing to do, perhaps, in the face of his sarcasm, and probably much too subtle, although people who had been close could often read hidden messages in a tone of voice.

Again she was surprised by the look of incredible scorn that filled Will's eyes. 'Well, at least you don't pretend any more,' he said scathingly.

'Pretend?' She frowned in puzzlement.

'That this new man in your life means more to you than your damn job.'

Hell! She'd forgotten that invention. It must have got back to Will with the speed of light. Straight from the woman she'd confided in probably.

Before she could find anything to say, Will said sharply, 'Who is this man?'

'No one.'

He gave a harsh laugh. 'Well, at least that's honest enough. What do you do—use him for sex when you're not away drumming up business for the first love of your life, the company?'

Paris flushed. 'I meant that he's no one you know.' His contempt sparked a flame of anger. 'And just what do you think gives you the right to be so damn rude?'

He suddenly lunged across the landing and caught her wrist. 'I have every right,' he said fiercely. 'You of all people should know that.'

She stared into his face and her anger fled. She wanted to ask him why it still mattered so much, whether it was because *she* still mattered, but was afraid of what he would say, that he would misunderstand her question. Devastated by his vehemence, she could only say in a husky, unsteady voice, 'Let me go, Will.'

The grip on her wrist tightened and for a moment his eyes threatened her, but then he stood back, dropping her arm. 'Sure.' His lips curled in disdain. 'Why the hell should I care if you louse up some other man's life?'

Turning away, he went quickly on down the stairs. Paris, stunned by that last, so very revealing remark, stood for a moment before taking a deep breath, then ran up towards her room.

It seemed to be her day for bumping into people on the landings. At the next one she literally bumped into another man—not so young as Will, and a stranger this time. She had been glancing down to watch Will as he reached and crossed the hall and hadn't noticed him.

'Oh! I'm sorry,' she exclaimed.

'My fault.' The stranger, of average height and with a pleasantly open face, put out an arm to steady her. 'No harm done, I hope?' he asked with an easy smile.

'No, of course not.'

Paris went to move round him but he said, 'You must be our late arrival, the missing member of the jury. Miss—Reid, isn't it?'

'Yes, that's right. Paris Reid.'

He didn't make the usual comment on the singularity of her name—which was a plus—instead saying, 'We were beginning to wonder if Ramsay had got to you before the police found you.'

'Oh, no. I've been away on business.' She hesitated, but the man seemed in no hurry to move on so she said, 'I'm sorry, I don't know who you are.'

'Ben Lucas.' He shook her hand. 'You probably don't recognise me because the last time we met I was wearing a wig.'

'A wig?' She looked in puzzlement at his full head of fair hair, then her brow cleared and she laughed. 'Oh, you mean you're a barrister. The wig-and-gown-type wig.'

'That's right.'

'Were you for the defence or the prosecution?'

'One of the barristers for the prosecution, I'm afraid.'

'Oh.' Paris's face clouded. 'So it was your colleague who was killed.'

'Yes, I'm afraid so, poor chap.'

The hotel-like atmosphere of the place and seeing Will again had driven the reason for their being here from Paris's mind. Now, realising in just how much danger Ben Lucas must have stood brought it back again and she gave a small shiver.

Ben saw it and recognised the cause. 'Look, there's plenty of time before dinner; how about a drink?'

'The bar won't be open yet, will it?'

'No, but I've got a bottle of very good whisky in my suite.'

'Suite?'

'Yes. Judge Paston and I were the first here so we got the choice of rooms. Come and see. I'm in one of the turrets.'

Paris hesitated for a moment, but after that encounter with Will she could do with a drink, and Ben seemed harmless enough. So she smiled, nodded, and went with him. They went up the stairs to her own floor, along the corridor and up another short flight set at an angle, then he unlocked a door in a thick round wall.

His suite was on two floors, the sitting-room on the lower, with a stone spiral stair in the thickness of the wall leading up to the room above. It was all most sumptuously furnished, the comfortable-looking sofa and two armchairs being upholstered in a soft green tartan. There was a music centre, television, bar and, best of all, a log fire blazing in the open hearth.

'Wow!' Paris looked round admiringly. 'This was worth getting here first for.'

Ben went over to the bar. 'Will Scotch do?'

'Please. On the rocks.' She sat in one of the armchairs and he brought the drink over to her, then sat on the sofa. 'I haven't seen you around today, have I?'

'No.' He gestured towards a desk on which there was a laptop computer and piles of folders. 'I've been working. I've too much on to be idle.'

'How do you get it in and out?'

'The police take it for me.'

'I wonder if they'd do that for me?' she mused. 'It's really frustrating not to be able to use the phone.'

'It has its advantages; at least you can work in peace and quiet.'

'Yes, I suppose there is that.' The whisky felt good in her throat. She gestured with the glass. 'Double malt?'

Ben nodded. 'The best.'

'We're in Scotland, aren't we?'

'It's better not to guess.'

She gave a small smile because he hadn't denied it, then said pensively, 'It will be the strangest Christmas I've ever had.'

'For all of us. But we shouldn't be lonely among so many—even if we have had to leave people we care about behind.'

Paris was immediately sympathetic. Ben must be in his forties, she guessed, and would probably have a family. 'Are you missing someone you care about?'

'No, I wasn't referring to myself—I'm a free agent. I was thinking of you.'

'Me?' She looked at him in surprise, wondering how, if he'd been here in his rooms all day, he could possibly have got to hear about her non-existent lover.

As if guessing her thoughts, Ben said, 'I'm afraid I overheard you talking to Will Brydon on the stairs. I thought I'd better not interrupt so I waited until you'd finished. You seem to have known him rather well.'

A tactful way of putting it, Paris thought. Momentarily she was angry that he had listened, but then gave a mental shrug; it was too late now, and what did it matter anyway? She said shortly, 'We were—we lived together for some time after the trial.'

'I see.'

'Do you?'

'I think so. You split up and now you've got someone else, but Brydon is still jealous.'

'Is that how it seemed to you?'

'Is that how it was?'

She raised an eyebrow. 'That sounds like a barrister's question.'

'Sorry.'

Swallowing her drink, Paris stood up and walked over to set her glass on the bar. 'Thanks for the whisky. I must go; I want to get ready for dinner.'

'Of course. I'll see you on your way.'

'I'm sure I can find it.'

But he insisted on coming with her. It would be just her luck, Paris though wryly, for Will to come along and find her coming out of Ben's room. But when Ben opened the door and led her out to the corridor it was empty; there was just a girl of about Paris's own age who was about to descend the far stairs.

Perhaps attracted by their voices, the girl glanced back. She was shorter than Paris, with a more curvy figure and curly dark hair. She hesitated for a moment as she glanced back at them, then went on her way.

Paris recognised her at once from the trial; she had been one of the witnesses for the prosecution—one of Ramsay's ex-girlfriends. Her name was Melanie Truscott—and something in the way she had looked at them made Paris instinctively aware that this was the girl whom Will had become friendly with. Turning to Ben, she saw the confirmation in his eyes, but still said, 'Her—and Will?'

He nodded. 'It would appear so.'

CHAPTER FOUR

PARIS went down to dinner at what she thought was the last minute, but she was still there before Will. He came in from the bar with Melanie Truscott and another couple when the first course had already started to be served, and the four sat together.

Glancing at them surreptitiously, Paris wondered just what Will saw in the other girl. Perhaps it was her availability; she had admitted to several affairs at the trial. Trying to recall the details, Paris remembered that the defence had tried to make out that the murder had been a crime of passion, caused by Ramsay finding out that Melanie had been unfaithful.

Surely Will couldn't be attracted to that kind of girl? Paris thought in amazement. He couldn't be that hard up. But then she bit her lip hard; it was none of her business whom he went with—not any more.

'Are you feeling unwell?'

The question came from a woman sitting on her left. Paris blinked and pulled herself back to the present. 'No, I'm fine, thank you.' She smiled. 'It's just that I was travelling nearly all last night and the day before and my lack of sleep is catching up with me.'

She used the same excuse to go straight to her room after dinner, but sat on the bed and watched television for some time before finally turning out the light and trying to sleep. After an hour of tormented wakefulness, Paris knew that there was no way she was going to sleep naturally, so took a couple of pills that put her out within minutes.

* * *

The next morning she woke feeling woolly-headed, as she always did after taking sleeping pills, but she managed to avoid Will that day, spending the morning writing Christmas cards—thoughtfully provided by the authorities—and the afternoon working out in the gym and swimming in the pool. The exercise made her feel much better, and she went up to her room to change for dinner with a far lighter step.

While she was changing the phone rang.

Paris stared at it; having been told not to use the phone she hadn't expected anyone to be able to call her. Tentatively she picked up the receiver. 'Yes?'

'Paris? This is Ben Lucas.'

She gave an inner laugh of rueful amusement at her own stupidity; she should have realised that this was also an internal phone. 'Hello, Ben.'

'Would you care to have a drink with me before dinner?'

'The malt hasn't run out yet, then?'

'No, but I thought maybe you'd prefer a drink in the bar.'

Paris hesitated, wondering why he'd suggested the bar. Was it, in the circumstances of their confinement, the equivalent of asking her for a date? So did she want to have a date with him, be seen with him by everyone else? And by everyone else, of course, she really meant Will. What would he think? And would he care when he was with the curvy Melanie? The thoughts raced through her mind, but then she told herself, What the hell! It's only a drink. So she said, 'Thanks. I'd like to. See you there in half an hour.'

The tartan bar in the hour before dinner proved to be a popular place. Nearly everyone seemed to be there.

Ben stood up and waved to her as Paris came into the room and she was aware of a great many eyes watching as she walked over to him. Probably because of the dark green velvet dress she was wearing, she thought. It had long sleeves but was cut low on her white shoulders, and it had a tight skirt that clung the way a skirt should. Her hair she had piled on top of her head above the chunky earrings that clinked a little when she moved. Quite why she had dressed up like this, Paris didn't know. Or maybe she did but didn't want to admit it to herself.

Ben's eyes went over her in satisfying admiration. 'Whisky again?' he asked.

'Somehow I don't think it would be as good as yours. I'll settle for gin and tonic, please.'

He went over to the bar and she sat down in the seat he'd saved for her at a small table for two, crossing her legs to show them to their best advantage. Looking round, she saw that Melanie was already there, sitting on one of the stools by the bar, but she was alone, or, at least, not with Will.

Wearing a red dress that stretched tight across her breasts, she was talking to some other women, three of whom Paris recognised as more of Ramsay's ex-girlfriends. Maybe they'd formed a mutual society, she thought flippantly.

Ben came back with her drink, looked her over again and said, 'Thank you,' as if he meant it.

She gave him an amused glance. 'For what?'

'For making my day.'

Paris smiled her acknowledgement of the compliment. 'Have you been working again?'

'Afraid so. How about you?' She told him, and he said with mock severity, 'You mean to say you didn't go to the talk this afternoon on making jewelry out of enamelled coins?'

There was such reproach in his voice that she laughed aloud. 'Don't knock it. You might end up doing exactly that one day.'

He raised his eyebrows high. 'God forbid,' he said fervently.

They both laughed, leaning towards each other in amusement. And it was at that moment Will walked into the room.

Paris knew at once that he was there. She didn't have to notice Melanie, who had been watching the door, suddenly sit up straight and smile a welcome—Paris had already sensed the sudden electricity in thê air. Without looking round, she leaned closer to Ben, still smiling, and said, 'So what are your hobbies?'

'I play cricket in the summer, squash in the winter, and bridge all the year.' He glanced round, saw Will going towards the bar and looked quickly back at Paris speculatively.

But she gave nothing away as she said, 'Well, at least you'll have plenty of bridge here, even if you haven't the others. Maybe you'll take up tatting or something.'

He gave her an old-fashioned look. 'I may be middle-aged compared with you, but I haven't got that far yet. What is tatting, anyway?'

'I've no idea,' Paris confessed. Will had come into her line of sight now and she deliberately let herself glance in his direction. For a moment their eyes met, but she let nothing show in hers before turning coolly away to resume her conversation. 'Are you good at bridge?'

'Fairly,' Ben admitted, having watched the little exchange.

'Oh.' She let disappointment show and sipped her drink.

'Why "Oh"?'

Paris gave a small shrug, then said with false reluctance, 'It was just that I don't know how to play bridge and I thought, if you had an odd half-hour to spare, you might teach me. But if you're good then you won't want to be bothered with a learner.'

Ben laughed. 'I'm afraid even someone as intelligent as you would find it difficult to pick up bridge in an odd half-hour. I've been playing for years and I'm still learning. But I'd be happy to try and teach you, of course.'

She had known that he would offer, but felt compelled to say, 'I don't want to take up too much of your time, especially when you're working during the day.'

'We'll start tonight,' he promised.

'I've lost track of the days. How many more to Christmas?'

'Five.'

'Five more shopping days to Christmas. I bet the high streets are doing a roaring trade right now,' she said on a wistful note.

'Having withdrawal symptoms?'

Paris laughed. 'Something like that. I didn't have much time for shopping while I was away.' Under her lashes she saw that Will had joined the group of women at the bar, buying them all a drink, and Melanie had a possessive hand on his arm as she talked to him, gesturing freely with the other.

Will seemed to be giving Melanie all his attention, but Paris knew that he was watching her too. It was a trick he had—seeming to concentrate on one thing but all the time being aware of what was going on around him. But he had never done that to her; when they'd been together she had had all his attention.

Turning to Ben, she saw that his eyes were on her face. 'Why did you invite me for a drink in here?' she asked abruptly.

'Isn't that what you wanted?'

'Why should it be?'

'So that you could let Brydon see that he isn't the only fish in the sea. To make him even more jealous, perhaps.'

He smiled. 'And so that you could put on that dress and look beautiful, show him just what he's missing.'

Her cheeks flushed a little. 'Those are—very acute observations.'

'True ones?'

'Perhaps. Partly.'

'Only partly?'

'I wore it for you too, and for myself.'

'What happened between you two? Did someone come between you?'

'I suppose you could say that,' Paris admitted, thinking of Emma and her poisonous tongue.

'Was it this man you're going with now?'

Paris hesitated, then said, 'There isn't another man. I just said that. I wanted to protect myself, I suppose.'

Looking at her, seeing the vulnerability in her eyes, Ben said, 'Now I understand.'

She smiled. 'Well, I'm glad someone does, because I certainly don't understand myself.'

'Don't you?' He gave her a quizzical look. 'Well, if you need a friend while you're here, I'm always available.' Seeing her hesitate, he added, 'Just a friend, Paris, nothing more. I don't want to complicate your life more than it is already. And besides, I'm a confirmed workaholic bachelor, than which there is nothing worse.'

That made Paris laugh, and she gave him a look of gratitude. The dinner gong sounded, people finished their drinks and made for the dining-room, the meal the high spot of the day, as meals always are in any institution, on any holiday.

They sat at a table with the judge and his wife and some other lawyers. The conversation was good, on an entirely different level from that of the table on which she'd sat last night, and Paris enjoyed herself. Afterwards she and Ben went to the card-room and Paris found out

that it was going to take her a whole lot longer to learn
bridge than she'd expected.

They didn't break up until gone midnight, when most
of the others had gone to their rooms. Ben escorted her
to her door but that was all; he merely said goodnight
and headed for his turret.

Her brain exhausted by trying to take so much in, Paris
slept like a log and woke feeling really refreshed. But
she didn't hurry to get up, instead turning over lazily,
only slowly becoming aware of the deadness of sound
from outside. Usually sounds echoed round the courtyard
but today there was nothing.

Getting out of bed, she went to the windows, drew
back the curtains and found that it had snowed in the
night. Quite heavily too—the wall looked to be several
inches higher and the greenness of the distant fir trees
was lost beneath their white caps.

Everyone was talking about the snow at breakfast. A
snowman-building competition was organised for the
children and people went off to their rooms after the
meal to find scarves, pipes, hats and gloves to decorate
them. Nearly everyone went out to watch and admire;
somebody started a snowball fight and even quite elderly
people joined in.

In the middle of the hilarity, during the most en-
joyable time they'd had there, Captain Waters came into
the courtyard, sought out a middle-aged couple who had
been Ramsay's neighbours, and who had given evidence
against him, and drew them back into the hotel.

A silence descended on all the other adults as they
waited in trepidation to find out what had happened.
They soon found out. The couple's house had deliberately been set on fire and petrol used to intensify the
flames, destroying their home and their two beloved cats,

which they had left behind to be looked after by their married daughter who lived nearby.

Lunch was a gloomy meal, especially after the merriment of the morning. Everyone was thinking about their own homes, wondering if they would be next. Captain Waters was besieged by people demanding protection for their houses, some even wanting to leave to go and guard the places themselves.

He calmed them as best he could, and pointed out that at least it proved that Ramsay was far away from the castle. Feeling overwhelmingly sorry for them, Paris went to her room and changed into jeans and sweater, boots and a thick jacket, then went outside.

The sun had come out, making the snow sparkle and crackle underfoot where it was still untrodden. The snowmen stood in a line, fat and jolly, given wide smiles by their proud creators.

The gates to the courtyard were locked, but through them she could see where an old moat had been partially filled in and the outline of shrubs and small trees planted on its edge. Beyond the moat there was a thicker wall and, at an angle, a gatehouse with rooms inside it, guarding another heavy wooden door. There was a light on in the gatehouse, which must always be gloomy with its small windows—sign of someone being on guard.

'Wishing you could leave?'

The snow had deadened his footsteps and she hadn't heard Will walk up to her. Paris caught her breath, then managed to shrug. 'There wouldn't be anything much to do.'

'The company's packed up for Christmas, has it?' he said with a definite sneer.

Paris hadn't meant that; she'd merely meant that she'd made no plans, that there wouldn't be much to do for a Christmas spent alone. She didn't bother to explain, just turned and walked on.

Will came to walk alongside her, his usual brisk stride slowed by the snow. For a few moments they paced along in silence, then he said, 'You've grown your hair.'

She turned quickly and surprised him in the act of lowering his ungloved hand and shoving it into his pocket, almost as if he had been about to touch her hair, which was hanging loose, blown by the slight breeze.

'Yes.' There was nothing else to say.

'And you look thinner.' That came out almost as an accusation.

'So do you.'

That surprised him. He blinked, then shrugged it off and said curtly, 'I see you haven't wasted any time in finding a gullible fool to entrap.'

'Nor have you,' Paris retaliated.

His eyes met hers and he frowned, looked as if he was about to say something, but then his jaw tightened and he looked away.

'Did you move back in with Emma?' he asked after a few moments. 'After you—left.'

'After you kicked me out? Isn't that what you mean?' He didn't answer and she said, 'No, of course not. She was the last person I'd have moved in with. If it hadn't been for her—' She stopped, unwilling to go over old ground.

'What were you going to say?'

'It doesn't matter.'

'It might.'

She glanced at him, but Will's face was still set and hard. Paris gave a wry smile. 'I don't think so.'

It seemed strange that he had asked her that, especially after all these years. He hadn't taken the trouble to enquire after her when he'd thrown her out, so why ask now? If he hadn't cared enough at the time then he surely couldn't care less now. It was one of the things that had added to her hurt then, and it had taken a long while to get over it. Paris found that she didn't want to talk about that time; it opened too many old wounds.

They turned the corner of the building and came in sight of the turret where Ben had his suite. Paris glanced up at his window, wondering whether he was there, whether he was watching them. But she gave Ben no more than a passing thought.

Abruptly she said, 'Do you think they will catch Ramsay soon? Have the police told you anything?'

'Nothing they haven't told anyone else. I know what he did today was dreadful, but the more criminal acts he commits, the more likely he is to make a mistake and get caught. At least he didn't hurt anyone this time.'

'He killed those poor cats,' Paris pointed out.

'They hardly matter compared with a human being.'

'Of course they matter.'

Will's mouth twisted. 'To *you*?'

His tone implied so much. The colour fled from Paris's face. She swung round to go back inside, desperate to get away from him.

But Will caught her arm. 'No, wait.'

'Damn you, let me go!'

'What's the matter—afraid to face up to your own guilt?' he bit out scornfully. 'You little coward.'

Suddenly she was angry, and fervently grateful for it. 'What the hell would you know?' She pushed him away. 'I've lived with what happened for three long years. I know everything there is to know about guilt. And about a hell of a lot of other emotions, too.'

Again she turned and tried to hurry away but the snow slowed her down and Will quickly caught up with her and barred her way. 'What are you trying to say?'

'Nothing!' Anger had brought colour back into her cheeks, made her green eyes flash fire. 'I didn't ask to come here and I certainly didn't want to. If seeing me again brings it all back, then I'm sorry, but there's nothing I can do about it. So just leave me alone. Keep away from me.'

'I can't!' Will spoke the words as if they were forced out of him.

For a moment the intensity in his voice brought them both up short. Then Paris gave a bitter laugh. 'Why? Wasn't throwing me out enough? Must I be punished all over again, is that it? Maybe you're a sadist; have you thought of that? Maybe you're getting a kick out of this.'

'Don't be ridiculous.'

'Then why are you being like this? Why do you keep on about the past?'

His face taut with emotion, Will burst out, 'Because I can't help it, damn it!'

Paris stared up at him, seeing the harsh bleakness in his eyes, feeling despair fill her heart. 'Oh, God, no,' she said on a breath of desolate consternation.

There was the sound of voices and some children came into sight. They were rolling a ball of snow before them, making it ever larger as they went, and had already achieved a ball that was almost as high as they were. A group of fathers followed, trying not to appear too eager to take over as soon as it was too big for the youngsters. Will had been about to reach for her again but he let his arm fall and Paris took the opportunity to leave him and run back to the castle.

She was desperate to be alone and ran up to her room, but it was being cleaned. 'Will you be long?' she asked the elderly cleaner.

'I've only just started,' the woman pointed out, in a Scots accent so broad that it would have left Paris in no doubt at all where they were if she hadn't already guessed.

She looked the kind of woman who was slow, thorough and not to be hurried. Abandoning the idea of finding solace in her room, Paris went to go downstairs again, but just couldn't face all the other people. So instead she went along the corridor to Ben's turret and climbed a narrow staircase that she'd noticed when she'd gone to his room for a drink. It was quite steep and there were no handrails.

At the top there was a narrow wooden door which was locked, but the key was hanging on a hook fixed in the wall. It was an old key, big and heavy, but turned easily in the lock. Opening the door, Paris found that it led outside again, onto the narrow parapet that encircled the roof.

She hesitated, and then, not wanting to get locked out, put the key in her pocket and went outside. The walkway was about two feet wide and a little slippery where the snow had melted in the sun. The parapet on her right, in the form of battlements, came up to her waist at the higher points, then only to her thighs, so she went carefully along. The roof to her left was of lead, its slope hidden from view below by the parapet.

Paris didn't know much about buildings and architecture, but it struck her that the construction of the roof didn't look that old and she realised for the first time that the building was a sham—Victorian Gothic masquerading as the real thing. It explained a lot: the good plumbing and the efficient central heating, the lack of draughts and the windows that gave plenty of light.

Continuing along the walkway, Paris came to the next turret with an identical door beside it. It was locked but her key fitted. Fascinated, she went inside, down another little staircase, round the curve of the turret, and found that to reach the next section of the roof she had to go up yet another staircase. How complicated. And just so that the architect hadn't had to break the line of his turrets at each corner of the building.

Instead of going on, Paris went back to her original walkway because it faced the sun. At least here she had found a hide-away, a place where she could be absolutely alone.

Looking down into the courtyard, she could see the place where she and Will had stood, the snow scuffed where he had come after her. She tried to remember the exact words of their conversation—no, confrontation had been more like it—but all she could remember was the intensity of it all.

Will should have forgotten by now. He had put the entire blame on her and got rid of her. So why hadn't he put it all out of his mind and started afresh? His vehemence had taken her aback; there had been a desperate kind of note in his voice that she couldn't fathom. But the guilt hadn't been his—in his eyes it had all been hers; so why should he feel like that? Paris found it impossible to understand him.

Only one thing was clear: if Will hadn't been able to forget what had happened after so long then he would definitely never be able to forgive her. In her heart maybe Paris had hoped that he would have relented by now, but it seemed that he still hated her. So there was nothing for it but to put Will out of her mind, out of her heart, to try and forget—but she had been trying to do just that for the last three years without any real success. So what hope was there for her? Paris thought tiredly.

She lifted her hands to press her temples, her head aching. The sun lost its battle with a dark grey cloud that suddenly took all the warmth out of the day. She shivered but stayed where she was, trying to work things out, wondering what she should do, wishing she was anywhere but there.

But then it began to snow again, so she turned and went back inside, remembering to lock the door behind her and hang the key on the hook where no inquisitive child could reach it.

After dinner that evening, Paris again had a bridge lesson, and this time another couple came to sit with them so that she could practise actually playing.

Numerate enough to count up to thirteen and blessed with a good memory, Paris took to the game like a duck to water. It had been years since she'd played any card game—not since before her parents had split up—but she enjoyed the challenge, and was grateful to concentrate entirely on the game and forget everything else. Or she did until she insisted that it was her turn to buy a round of drinks.

When she went into the bar she found Will sitting in a corner with Melanie. There were drinks on the table in front of them but it seemed that the other girl had already had quite a few because she was giggling and leaning heavily against Will.

Maybe she was the kind of woman who got amorous after she'd had several drinks and Will was taking advantage of it, Paris thought cynically. He certainly didn't seem to mind; his long-lashed grey eyes were laughing down at the girl in amusement. They both glanced up as Paris walked in, and Melanie's mouth creased into a definite smile of malicious triumph.

Paris looked quickly away, but there had been no mistaking that look; the other girl obviously knew that Will and she had had a relationship in the past. And there was only one person who could have told her.

Paris's first feeling was of betrayal; how *could* Will have told anyone else, let alone a girl like that? And what else had he told Melanie? Had he told her that he believed Paris to have had an abortion, too? Was that going to be passed round for everyone to gossip over?

'Yes, miss? Miss?' The bartender raised his voice and Paris realised that he was waiting for her order.

She gave it and took the drinks into the card-room on a tray, careful not to look in Will and Melanie's direction as she went out.

After that she didn't play so well and soon Ben said that he thought she'd had enough. The other couple went up to their room and Ben said, 'Would you like to go into the bar for a nightcap?'

'No, let's stay here.'

'I take it that means Will Brydon is in the bar?'

She didn't deny it, just leaned her elbows on the table, rested her chin on her hands and said, 'Tell me about yourself, Ben.'

'What do you want to know?'

'Do you believe in love?'

His eyebrows rose. 'I didn't expect that question. What makes you ask?'

'You're a criminal lawyer; you must have experience of life with a capital L, have met so many people, heard so many stories.'

'That doesn't necessarily mean I have all the answers. I certainly believe in the power of attraction, if that's what you mean.'

'No, I know there's that. I mean real love—the kind you read about that lasts for ever.'

'Oh, yes, I suppose I do. I've seen people who've stood by their loved one through the most terrible times. Take Noel Ramsay, for instance—he seemed to have the knack of making women fall in love with him. A couple of them were reluctant to testify against him, even though he'd got angry and beaten them up. They wouldn't say anything against him until they found out about his other women.'

'Was Melanie Truscott one of the reluctant ones?' Paris couldn't help asking.

'I think she was at first, yes,' Ben admitted, watching her.

'She seems to have got over him completely now,' Paris remarked on an unknowingly acid note.

Ben's eyes flicked to her face, then he said, 'Yes, most of the women have. Though I think they may have more reason to be afraid of Ramsay than most of us.'

'Why?'

'Ramsay has a warped mind; he probably thinks that they betrayed him, and so he would want to be revenged on them more than anyone else. Don't forget that one of the girls has completely disappeared. The police have found no trace of her and must be pretty convinced by now that Ramsay got to her and has killed her.'

'He's such an evil man,' Paris burst out. 'Why on earth were they stupid enough to let him get away?' They were silent for a moment, each thinking the same thoughts, but then she said, 'I wish they'd hurry up and catch him.'

'You're in a hurry to leave?'

'Yes. Aren't you?'

Ben shrugged. 'Not desperate, no. I'm getting a lot of work done and I've nowhere else much to go for Christmas, so I'm happy to spend it here, among friends. Although I know you don't agree.'

Paris sighed. 'I wouldn't mind at all if Will weren't here. But as it is...' She shrugged.

'Is there no hope of the two of you getting back together?'

'Oh, no, none.' Her answer was decisive.

'Why not?'

'There are too many old emotions standing in the way.'

'I see.' Ben yawned and got to his feet. 'I think it's time I turned in.'

They walked companionably up the stairs; avoiding the lift had become a habit now. Someone in the lounge was playing a Christmas song on the piano and people were joining in, forgetting their fears. The sound followed them, hid the noise of their step on the carpeted stairs. Maybe that was why Will and Melanie didn't hear them.

The two of them were standing just outside an open door a short way from the staircase on the second floor, locked in a close embrace. Paris came to an abrupt stop, not wanting to attract their attention by walking by. But she needn't have worried; Melanie broke away and with a slow, sex-filled laugh, caught hold of Will's arm and drew him into the room.

Paris immediately strode quickly to the next flight and began to climb it rapidly, Ben having to hurry to keep up. 'I take it that was Will's room?' she said shortly.

'No, I think it was hers.'

Paris frowned, something momentarily troubling her mind, but she pushed it aside, too angry and humiliated to care. Her goodnight to Ben was curt and she would have gone straight into her room, but he caught her hand.

'Maybe he's just doing it to make *you* jealous,' he suggested.

'No, he doesn't care enough for that.'

'Of course he does.'

She turned on him angrily. 'Are you so blind? Will doesn't care about me—he hates me. Hates me so much he can't leave it alone!' She bit her lip, her hand clenching within his, the pain she was feeling impossible to hide.

Ben stared at her, then said awkwardly, 'Look, don't try and bottle things up. That's no good, you know.'

His kindness made Paris angry with herself. She collapsed against the wall, saying, 'God, I'm being really rotten to you, aren't I? Just forget about me, Ben. I'm a lost cause.'

'Nonsense. You're a beautiful, intelligent woman. And maybe you deserve someone better than Will Brydon.'

She looked at him for a moment without really seeing him, then shook her head in infinite sadness. 'No, it's the other way round.' Ben went to speak but she raised her hand in a small gesture to silence him, turned and went into her room.

Again she lay awake, unable to stifle the jealousy that tore at her heart. She had no right to feel that way, she knew, but could do nothing about it.

Will certainly hadn't needed any persuading to go with Melanie. He had allowed her to pull him into her room without even the slightest hint of resistance. But then, why should he resist? When a pretty girl made it obvious that she was available he'd have to be a fool not to take what was offered.

Pictures of the two of them in bed together tortured her mind, became unbearable. Getting out of bed, Paris scrabbled for the bottle of sleeping pills. She ought not to take so many of these, she thought, but she just had to sleep; she couldn't stand her own vivid imagination any longer.

She took two, got back into bed again, but it was something else now that niggled at her mind, and it was just as she was fading into oblivion that she remembered. The first time she had seen Melanie the girl had been going downstairs from this floor. So if Melanie's room was on the second floor, what had she been doing on the third?

Waking late the next morning, Paris didn't bother to go down to breakfast, and she stayed in her room most of the day. When she finally went down just in time for dinner she found that a huge Christmas tree had been set up in the hall. Everyone seemed to have gone into the dining-room already, but she stopped to admire it. It was hung with colourful bows and decorations, and twinkled with flashing lights and tinsel. A masterpiece of a tree!

As she stood admiring it, Will came down the stairs and walked up to her. Paris saw him and forced herself not to walk away, not to show any emotion.

'The children did it this afternoon,' he told her. 'They had a wonderful time.'

'It's magnificent.'

Will was standing with his hands in his pockets, spoiling the line of his well-cut suit. Glancing at her, he said, 'You haven't been around today.'

Hiding her surprise at his noticing, Paris said as casually as she could, 'No, I've been catching up on some chores, writing letters, washing my hair. You know.'

'I like it longer.' This time he openly reached up to touch it.

Suddenly angry, Paris swung away from him, her hair swirling. 'I don't give a damn what you like or don't like,' she said forcefully.

Will gave a small gasp. 'What the hell was that for?'

'Concentrate on one girl at a time, why don't you?'

His eyes narrowed. 'Why should you care what I do, who I'm with?'

Angry with herself, she tried her best to retrieve the situation. 'I don't. I just want you to get away from me. Go back where you're welcome—more than welcome, by the looks of it.' And, to her consternation, she found herself adding, 'You and all her other men.'

'What's that supposed to mean?' Will's hands were out of his pockets now, were on his hips, and he was glaring at her. It was too late to take it back now, and anyway, she didn't want to. Lowering her voice, Paris said forcefully, 'You used to be more fastidious.'

'Fastidious? Because I chose to live with you—is that what you mean? Do you think yourself so moral, then? What about the way you're going around with Ben Lucas when you already have a boyfriend tucked away somewhere?'

'Ben is just being friendly, and you know it. I only met him a few days ago, for heaven's sake. Not that knowing someone only a short time seems to have caused *you* any qualms,' she added nastily.

Will leaned towards her, his strong jaw jutting forward. 'Has it occurred to you that Melanie's morals might be a damn sight more honest than yours? OK, maybe she sleeps around and you don't, but does that make you better than her, after what you did? Well, does it?'

CHAPTER FIVE

SO THEY were back to the same thing again, at the same point as they had been three years ago. The colour flooded from Paris's face as she realised that this was how it would always be whenever she saw Will, whenever they talked. Although, talking didn't really come into it, because all they'd done since she'd been here was tear each other to pieces.

She turned blindly and went to hurry away, but Will caught her elbow. 'The dining-room is the other way.'

'I'm not hungry.'

'You didn't come down to lunch. You've got to eat,' he said with a rough edge to his voice.

'No, what I need is a drink,' Paris said on an unnatural laugh. And, pulling herself free of his hold, she headed for the bar.

Will looked at her uneasily for a moment, then gave a small shrug and went into the dining-room.

The bar was completely empty, the grille pulled down over the bar counter and the barman gone to have his own meal, presumably. Paris didn't much care. She went into the card-room, picked up a pack and, sitting down at one of the tables, began to play patience. Her mind wasn't on it; she stared moodily down at the cards, wishing for what seemed like the millionth time that she could get away from Will, away from the castle.

There was a movement by the door and she looked up. It was Will. He paused in the doorway for a moment, his hand against the frame, then came into the room.

In his other hand he carried a tray with a bowl of soup, a roll and a glass of wine.

'Here.' He brushed the cards aside and put the plate in front of her.

She gazed up at him for a moment, then said huskily, 'Thanks.'

Paris expected him to go then, but instead Will sat down next to her and broke and buttered the roll. She watched him, his long, deft capable hands. It reminded her of so many other times, when they'd been together, when she had watched him working at some task, fascinated by his efficiency. The memory was raw hurt and she almost hated him for bringing it back. 'Why?' she said shortly.

'Just eat, Paris.'

'I don't want your pity, damn you!'

'Good, because you're not getting it. All you're getting is a bowl of soup. So eat.'

Strangely she saw the funny side of that and gave a low chuckle. Picking up the spoon, she took a couple of mouthfuls, then said, almost conversationally, 'I thought I knew you. But I don't. I didn't when we were together and I still don't.'

'You certainly didn't know me then.'

She glanced at him. He was leaning back in his chair, one leg crossed over the other knee—the way men sit when they're relaxed—and his hands were in his pockets. His face showed no emotion, could have been that of a stranger, but it had seldom pulled at her heart so much.

The soup was Scotch broth, very thick, a meal in itself. Paris took another couple of spoonfuls before she said reflectively, 'I think I did know you better then—knew you instinctively—but I was persuaded otherwise.'

'Who by?'

She shook her head and picked up a piece of bread. 'It doesn't matter.'

'I suppose I needn't have asked; it was that bitch Emma, wasn't it?' Paris didn't answer and he said grimly, 'Are you still friendly with her? Do you see her?'

'Oh, no. I haven't seen her since I was instrumental in getting her fired.'

Will straightened, his eyes on her face. 'And just how did you do that—and why?'

Paris hesitated, then said on a rueful sigh, 'I didn't realise it for a long time, but Emma was frightened to death of getting old. It made her dreadfully jealous of any younger girl she saw as a possible threat to her own job, her position in the firm. So she used to get them to leave in a very subtle way.

'First she'd pretend to be very friendly and let them share her flat, offer to take over their best accounts for a while if they were on holiday—or serving on a jury, as I was. Then she'd lie and make up excuses so she could keep the accounts, then kick the girl out of the flat and make her life unbearable at work until she either left or got fired.'

Breaking off another piece of bread, Paris paused, remembering, then said on a small laugh, 'She'd done that to two other girls before me, only it didn't work with me because I had you. I moved in with you and I managed to find some new accounts. But then I was stupid enough to play into her hands by confiding in her about—about being pregnant.'

Paris bit her lip, but went on, 'Afterwards, she told everyone I'd had an abortion, made sure they talked about it. I think she even urged that disgusting man to find you, tell you.' She fell silent, looking down at her plate, no longer eating.

'So what happened?' Will demanded.

She flicked him a glance. 'After you—after we split up, work was hell—Emma saw to that. She—' Paris broke off; she wasn't looking for his pity or even sympathy, so instead she said, 'But it was all I had left so I clung to it. I was determined not to let her win. Then I found out that she'd done the same kind of thing before, so I traced the other two girls and we got together, put our cases to the management and threatened to sue for harassment. That forced them to look into it for themselves.'

She began to eat again. 'It was surprisingly easy when it came to it. Maybe the management had become aware of what Emma was doing; maybe they just wanted to be rid of her. Anyway, one day she was there, the next she was gone.'

'How did she make your life such a hell at work?'

'That hardly matters now.'

'Doesn't it?'

'No, it's over. And it wouldn't matter to you anyway.'

But Will surprised her by saying, 'Yes, it would. I'm glad it happened, that you did it. She was a bitch.'

'You sound very certain.'

'I am. She tried to get me to take her to bed, one night when you were abroad at a conference.'

Paris turned to stare at him. 'Really? Why didn't you ever tell me?'

'Because she was supposed to be your closest friend. Because she threatened, if I said anything to you, to tell you that it had been the other way round; that *I'd* tried to make it with her.'

'Do you mean to say that she just came round to our place and asked you to go to bed with her?'

'No, she wasn't quite that blatant. She phoned late at night and said that something had gone wrong with her central-heating boiler, that it was making a terrible noise and she was afraid it was going to blow up. I told her to phone a plumber but she said she'd tried and no one would come out. So I didn't have much choice but to go round there.'

'And?' Paris said when he paused.

'Finish your soup.' She arched her brows impatiently but ate the last few spoonfuls, and only then did Will go on. 'When I arrived she greeted me at the door wearing a nightdress and negligée, all black lace and a lot of cleavage, and said the noise from the boiler had suddenly stopped. I went to go home but she begged me to stay for a while in case it started up again. I looked at the boiler but I couldn't find a thing wrong with it. It was then, just in case I hadn't already got the idea, that she began to come on strong.'

Paris picked up the glass of wine and sipped it slowly. 'What did you do?'

Will shrugged. 'What do you expect? I told her that even if I wasn't already living with you, with a girl I was crazy about, she'd be the last woman I'd ever want to go to bed with. Then I pushed her aside and walked out.'

At his description of her, Paris's fingers had tightened on her glass, but now she gave a sigh of surprised comprehension. 'Now I know why she hated me so much! I thought it was just because of work that she had it in for me, but I didn't know the "woman scorned" bit came into it as well. Maybe if I had I'd have been on my guard against her.'

'Are you saying I should have told you?' Will's lips thinned. 'That everything that happened was my fault?'

'No, of course not.' She gave a definite shake of her head. 'Anyway, it's all in the past now. Over. "Might have beens" and "if onlys" are just a waste of time—and heartache.'

His voice softening a little, Will said, 'Where did you go after we split?'

'Oh, I found a place. I got by,' she said lightly, and quickly changed the subject. 'How about you? Are you still working for the same firm?'

'No, I got restless. I spent some time in America, Hong Kong, Tokyo, learning the foreign money markets, widening my field.'

'A good career move.'

His lips twisted into a cynical smile. 'That wasn't why I did it.'

She understood at once and raised troubled eyes to his. 'I wished we'd talked—before—before—'

'Before I threw you out?' Will stood up and picked up her tray. 'It wouldn't have made any difference. I couldn't bear to be near you after what you did.'

Her face shadowed and she looked away, trying to hide the pain that knifed into her heart. That hadn't been what she'd meant but she didn't correct him. After a long moment she said, 'Well, I'm glad we've talked now.'

Will laughed mirthlessly. 'At least for once we didn't tear into one another.'

He carried the tray back to the dining-room and Paris watched him go, thinking how very wrong he was.

Later she sat in the bar with Ben and some other people, but pleaded a headache as an excuse for not playing bridge.

'Maybe you're coming down with a cold or something,' one woman said sympathetically. 'You must have an early night and dose yourself up. You don't want to miss the party tomorrow.'

'What party?'

'Haven't you heard? A couple of people are sharing a birthday, and they decided they'd like to have a party followed by carol singing. Can you sing?'

'Definitely not,' Paris said firmly. 'So don't get any ideas.'

Ben laughed. 'You'll get roped into doing something soon—you'll see. I've been asked to help accompany the singers on guitar.'

'You play the guitar?'

'Product of a misspent youth. Why are you so surprised?'

'I don't know; I suppose because you seem so wrapped up in your work.'

'Well, I won't be wrapped up in it tomorrow. It's the weekend and I'm taking a couple of days off.'

'Good for you.' Paris got to her feet, said goodnight, and left them as they pulled their chairs up to a table to start a rubber of bridge.

A film was being shown on the video, somebody had organised a debate on the government's controversial road-improvement schemes, and there were lots of people in the bar and lounge. The younger children, tired after another day of playing in the snow, were safely asleep in bed. It seemed that Paris was the only person going up to her room so early.

The lift was on the ground floor and for a moment she was tempted to take it, but she'd had no exercise that day so she went up the stairs instead. She saw no one until she reached her own floor, then a movement at the end of the corridor caught her eye. She came quickly up the last few steps and was in time to see a woman getting into the lift. Paris was pretty sure that it was Melanie Truscott; she recognised her figure, the dress she was wearing and the large handbag she always carried, although she didn't actually see her face.

She stood on the landing, remembering that she'd seen Melanie up here before. Was there some lone man on this floor that she visited? If so, it was a strange time to do so. Maybe it was one of their guards. Paris knew that Captain Waters had a room up here—perhaps some of the other men did too. She wouldn't have been at all surprised to know that Melanie had more than one man on a string, although how any woman would need another man when she had someone as virile as Will Paris couldn't think.

The familiar flame of jealousy hit her and she strode towards her room, but slowed as she noticed some marks on the carpet. Bending down, she touched them and found that they were wet. From someone's shoes, obviously. And Melanie had been the only person up here.

Gripped by curiosity, Paris followed the marks to the next corner turret along from the one with Ben's room in it and up one of the small staircases that led onto the roof. The wet marks were very definite here on the stone steps and looked to be from a woman's shoes; they were too small to be made by a man's, especially by the boots favoured by their police guards. But surely Melanie couldn't have gone outside tonight? It must be icily cold out there. Paris hesitated, then unlocked the door and opened it a little way.

Immediately the wind hit her, even before the cold caught at her breath. She gasped and began to shiver in her short-sleeved dress as she stepped onto the parapet. It was pitch-dark; the curtains of the windows of the castle were all drawn so there wasn't even any reflected light. She must be mistaken, Melanie couldn't possibly have come out here; she'd have frozen to death in no time.

Afraid that she'd freeze herself, Paris turned to go back inside just as a fresh gust caught her. Instinctively she put out a hand to steady herself against the turret wall—and gave a scream of fright as she touched something furry and warm.

Her cry was lost on the wind, which was just as well as only a second later she realised that what she had touched was only a coat. A very thick anorak with a hood was hanging from a nail in the wall, protected from the wind and rain by the overhanging circular roof of the tower. It was lined with fur that was still warm from human contact, and it was this that Paris had inadvertently touched. One of the guards must have left it here. Or Melanie.

That thought came uneasily into her mind. What could the other girl possibly want up here at night? But then it occurred to Paris that she too had come up here—looking for solitude, wanting to be alone. But that had been in daytime and because her own room hadn't been available. It all seemed strange, wrong.

Troubled, Paris went back inside and locked the door, then rubbed her arms to restore some warmth in them as she walked to her room. Once there, she went to pick up the phone to call Captain Waters, to tell him what she'd seen, but hesitated with her hand over the receiver.

What if there was some perfectly innocent explanation? There could be. Maybe Melanie was an amateur astronomer or something. She would look an absolute fool if that turned out to be the case. And, again, she hadn't actually seen the other girl's face, couldn't definitely swear that it was her, even though she was sure in her own mind.

But what finally made Paris decide not to phone was the thought that it might be put down to jealousy on her part because Will and Melanie were having an affair. All the other jurors would know that Will and she had been close at the time of the trial, and she was certain that the police had looked into their background and knew that they had once lived together. No, there were too many things against it; she would wait until tomorrow and perhaps talk it over with Ben first, see what he advised.

Paris woke early the next morning and, too restless to go to sleep again, went down to the gym to work out, and afterwards swam for half an hour in the pool. There were showers in the pool area which she used before going in to the dining-room. Ben wasn't there, but that wasn't unusual; he seldom bothered with breakfast.

After the meal Paris hesitated, wondering whether to go up to his room to see him, but not wanting to disturb him if he was sleeping late. In the end she compromised by writing a note saying that she wanted to see him which she sealed in an envelope and pinned on the notice-board in the hall, where he would be sure to see it when he came downstairs. If the note was still there in an hour, she decided, she would phone his room and get him to come down and talk to her.

As she pinned the note on the board, the front doors were pushed open and three grinning policemen in plain clothes came in, each carrying two large, heavy sacks. They looked like new forms of Father Christmas in their boots and duffel-coats and with the snow clinging to them.

'Post!' they called out. 'The mail has arrived.'

People gathered round them excitedly, adults as well as children, all eager for this link with the outside world. The policemen emptied the sacks onto a table in the hall, creating a great pile of letters and parcels which had been held back at all their local sorting offices and collected for them by the police. They sorted the parcels first and Paris noted that there were two for her, but to everyone's surprise one of the men took them all away again, going through the door into the kitchen area.

'We just have to check the parcels,' another man explained.

The letters were given out, most of them white-enveloped Christmas cards—whole wads of them to some people. The word had gone round and people were coming from all directions, laughing and talking, the arrival of the mail cheering them all.

Will walked in with Melanie at his side, and Paris tried not to wonder if they'd spent the night together. Some people took their post away to open but the majority were still gathered in the hall when there was the unmistakable sound of an explosion from the basement.

Some women screamed, others grabbed their children to them, and everyone grew tense, their faces full of alarm. Will had just gone forward to collect his mail; he took a step backwards, somehow placing himself between Paris and the door to the kitchens, whether accidentally or on purpose she didn't know. They were all gazing towards the door, appalled at what might have happened. The two policemen dropped the letters they were holding and ran out, followed closely by Captain Waters who came tearing across the hall. It was almost ten unbearably long minutes before he came back again, his face grave.

First he suggested that the mothers take the children away, and when they'd gone he said, 'I'm afraid there was a small bomb in one of the parcels. But no one has been hurt. The man who opened it was wearing gloves and protective clothing; he's quite all right. And no damage has been done downstairs.' He smiled at them and said in a falsely cheerful voice, 'Don't worry, you'll all get your Christmas dinner.'

One woman, her voice trembling, said, 'The—the parcel—who was it sent to?'

The captain hesitated, then said, 'It was addressed to Melanie Truscott.'

Paris's eyes swung swiftly to the other girl, saw the stunned amazement on her face, and then she swayed, about to faint. Several arms went out to her, but it was Will who stepped swiftly to her side and caught her as she fell.

Picking Melanie up in his arms, Will carried her into the lounge and laid her down on one of the sofas. Someone produced some smelling salts and soon Melanie was coming round. She sat up and seemed dazed, saying,

'I can't believe it. I can't believe it.' Then she started to cry and turned her head into Will's shoulder. He put his arms round her, comforting her as one would someone close.

Several people looked on sympathetically, but most people were still in the hall. They stood around, all of them talking about the letter bomb, their voices subdued, and some—mostly the parents—were looking angry, saying that the post should have been inspected before it was brought there.

One man who had three small children to whom several parcels had been addressed started to accuse Captain Waters of not taking sufficient care, of not guarding them properly. It was a natural reaction, Paris supposed; they'd all been scared, and what if the bomb had been bigger? What if someone had been killed?

Captain Waters called for silence and raised his voice to address them. 'I'm sorry that you've all had a scare. In future all the post will be checked before it's brought here.

'But can't you see what Ramsay is doing? He knows that you're all in a safe place. He can't get at you. So he's trying to make you panic, to make you worry about your homes, and perhaps scare you into going back to them. But you must trust the police to take care of them for you. If you leave here your lives will be in danger. I can't stress that enough. So please, try to forget this has happened. We're having a party tonight; let's look forward to that.'

It was sensible advice but not that easy to take, although they tried. The crowd began to break up, several people going into the ballroom to practise for the carol concert.

Paris turned away and saw Ben standing on the edge of the crowd. He was holding a guitar in one hand and her note in the other. She went over to him and by tacit consent they moved away from the hall and went to the empty card-room. As on most mornings, the sun was shining, the rays streaming through the windows. The cleaners must have been in here recently, because dust motes still danced in the air.

'Did you hear what happened?' Paris asked.

'Yes.'

'You said Melanie would be high on Ramsay's hit list.'

'Sending her letter bombs won't flush her out. It will make her all the more determined to stay here.'

'She seemed so amazed that she should have received it—completely stunned,' Paris said with a frown.

'Any one of us would have been.'

'Yes, I suppose so.'

Ben gestured with the note he was holding. 'What did you want to see me about that was so important?'

'Oh, that.' Paris pulled herself out of her abstraction. Her suspicions about Melanie now seemed incredibly silly. Whatever Melanie had been up to on the roof—if it had been her—it couldn't possibly have anything to do with Ramsay, not after the letter bomb. Her faint and the amazement afterwards had obviously been genuine; no one could be such a good actress that she could fake reactions like that. 'I just wondered if you'd give me another bridge lesson today,' she said lamely.

Ben looked surprised. 'Of course. But I have to practise with the carol singers this morning. In fact I'm late already.'

'I hardly think anyone will notice this morning.'

Ben went off but Paris didn't follow him, instead going to sit on the deep sill of one of the windows, her back against the wall, her legs stretched out before her, one knee bent a little.

She was still wearing the tight black leggings that she had worn in the gym, and over them a long white sweater, belted at the waist. Her hair was tied back in a pony tail, but several tendrils had come loose to caress her cheeks and throat. Leaning her head back, Paris closed her eyes, soaking up the reflected sun, which was bright on her face.

Maybe she dozed a little; maybe she was in that dream-like state between sleeping and waking. When she opened her eyes, languidly lifting her lids, she certainly thought that she was dreaming. Will stood nearby, looking down at her with oh, such a look on his face. Tenderness, desire, regret—they were all written there and plain to read. His eyes were as she'd so often known them when they'd been together—so warm, so dark with open need.

Paris's lips parted and she sat up eagerly, blinking against the sun. And then everything was suddenly back to normal, back in focus. Will was there all right—she hadn't imagined that—but his face was withdrawn, cool, as it always was when he looked at her now. In his hands he carried her parcels, obviously having been opened and resealed with sticky tape.

'The rest of the parcels were brought up and everyone collected them except you.'

'Thanks for bringing them.'

'It was thought better not to leave them just sitting there; it would remind everyone of what happened.'

'Oh, I see.' She took the parcels from him, glanced at the writing on the labels and saw that they were from her parents. 'How's Melanie?' she asked a little stiffly.

'All right now, I think. She had a large brandy and went up to her room.'

Paris glanced at him from under her lashes, wondering why he hadn't gone with her. 'She seemed very shaken,' she remarked.

'Yes.' Will gave a small frown. 'Didn't she.' But then he shrugged. 'I suppose we all think that nothing could ever happen to us, that it's always the other person.'

'But she's had experience of Ramsay before,' Paris pointed out, and couldn't help adding, 'Intimate experience.'

Will's mouth twisted slightly, but he said, 'Yes, the poor girl has really suffered at his hands. One has to feel sorry for her.'

'Perhaps she just has rotten judgement,' Paris pointed out tartly.

His smile became sarcastic as he looked down at her. 'We all make mistakes in judgement. You, above all, should know that.'

There was nothing to say to that. Paris's hands gripped the parcels and she looked away. Will turned to go but just then Gwenda Paston came into the room.

'Oh, there you are, Paris. I've been looking for you. We've had the most wonderful idea to take the children's minds off that stupid incident this morning. We're going to have a pantomime.'

'Really?' Paris tried to concentrate. 'Yes, that's a great idea. Which one?'

'*Snow White and the Seven Dwarfs*, so that the children can play the dwarfs. The others who want to take part can be villagers or fairies or something. There'll be lots of work to do and I shall need everyone's help.'

'Of course. I'll be glad to. But there's hardly any time left before Christmas; how will you be ready in time?'

'Oh, it won't be before Christmas; pantomimes are best as after-Christmas treats, don't you think? But we must start rehearsing and planning straight away.' She turned to Will. 'Now what are you good at? Carpentry, electrics, painting? Can you turn your hand to any of those?'

'I can try,' Will said in amusement at being press-ganged.

'He's good at painting,' Paris put in. 'He could do your scenery for you.'

Will gave her a look, but didn't argue when Mrs Paston greeted the information with enthusiasm. 'That's marvellous; I was beginning to worry about that. You must get together with the people I'm organising to build the scenery, tell them what you want when you've read the script.'

'You already have a script?' Will asked with a grin of admiration.

'It's being worked on,' Mrs Paston said grandly, then laughed and said in an entirely different tone, 'Anyway, everybody knows the story of Snow White; all we have to do is remember and write it down.'

'How can I help?' Paris asked.

'Why, you're going to be the most important person in the pantomime. I took one look at your legs in those woollen tights this morning and knew at once that you must be our principal boy.' She appealed to Will. 'Doesn't she have the most gorgeous legs?'

To Paris's embarrassment they both looked assessingly at her legs. Will nodded. 'She certainly does—and long too. Ideal for a principal boy, I'd say.'

'Exactly,' Mrs Paston said with satisfaction.

'But I can't,' Paris objected.

'Nonsense. You'll be ideal. And you mustn't worry about not having acted or anything before; we're all amateurs, you know.'

'No, you don't understand—'

'She's probably worried that she'll have to sing,' Will broke in, imps of mischief dancing in his eyes. 'She can't, you see.'

'You sound very sure.'

'I am. I've heard her, especially in the bath, and, believe me, you wouldn't want her to try.'

Paris, her cheeks pink, gave him an indignant look, but said, 'It's quite true. I'm afraid you'll have to find someone else.'

Mrs Paston had been looking at Will in some surprise, but turned again to Paris. 'No, I won't, because it doesn't really matter that you can't sing. One of the women has a wonderful voice but a terrible figure; she can sing the songs in the wings and you can mime to them. So that's settled. Now I have to persuade someone to play the wicked queen. I wonder...

She went to turn away but Paris pushed her parcels aside and got quickly to her feet. 'No! I'm sorry, but you don't understand. I *can't* be in the pantomime.'

The sharpness of her tone made the older woman turn to look at her more closely. 'Are you shy or something?'

'No, it isn't that. I'll gladly help you with the preparations until Christmas, but I can't take part because I won't be here after that. I'm leaving.'

'Leaving? But you can't! I mean—what if Ramsay hasn't been caught?'

Paris was aware of Will staring at her intently. Ignoring him, she said, 'I shall still be leaving. I'm sorry. If I can help in any other way, I will, of course.'

Mrs Paston frowned, not understanding. 'But how can you possibly leave? The police—surely they won't let you?'

Unable to explain, especially with Will standing there, Paris said, 'It's all arranged.' She picked up her parcels. 'Excuse me.'

Will went to stop her as she hurried out of the room but Mrs Paston spoke to him and he had to turn back.

Carrying a parcel under each arm, Paris ran to the hall and up the stairs. She had no doubt that Mrs Paston was asking Will what she'd meant, and was also sure that he would try to find out. That was why she locked her door when she reached her room.

Sitting on the bed, she began to unwrap her parcels. There was a card and letter enclosed in the one from her mother, with lots of photographs of her family—of

Paris's stepfather and her half-sister and brother, both quite a lot younger than herself. She began to read the letter, and when a knock sounded at the door she didn't answer it.

The knock came again, louder and more imperative this time, but still she ignored it. Then came Will's voice. 'Paris I know you're in there. Open the door.'

She sat silently. He banged impatiently on the panel, making the oak door rattle, then he must have gone away, because he didn't knock again. Two minutes later the phone rang. It went on ringing until at last she could stand it no longer. With a curse she picked up the receiver, fully intending to just lay it by the phone, but she heard Will's voice say loud and clear, 'Paris, if you don't speak to me I'll come up and break your door down.'

'All right! So I'm listening,' she said shortly.

'Why wouldn't you open your door?'

'Possibly because I don't want to talk to you.'

'You can't hide away for ever. What's this about you leaving?'

'You heard what I said.'

'I suppose it's some conference you feel you can't live without attending,' Will said in disgust.

'You can think what you like.'

'You mean it isn't?' he pounced.

'I'm not going to tell you, Will, so just drop it, will you?'

'No, I damn well won't! You're not going anywhere until Ramsay is caught, do you hear me?'

'Yes, I hear you,' Paris answered shortly. 'And anyone hearing you might just think that you cared.'

There was silence at the other end of the line as he was brought up short. She put down the phone and it didn't ring again.

Will was right, of course: she couldn't hide away for ever. She went down to lunch and found him hanging around in the hall, apparently glancing through a newspaper. But he put it down immediately when he saw her and took a firm hold of her arm. 'You've some explaining to do,' he said shortly, and steered her into the nearest empty room, shutting the door firmly behind them and then leaning on it.

'Now,' he said curtly, 'I want to know why you intend to leave here.'

'It's none of your business.'

'Don't try that one because it won't work. Why, Paris?'

Still defiant, she said, 'What's it to you? Why all this anxiety to know?'

But he'd had time to think up an answer to that one and said, 'It's of concern to us all, not just me. Don't you realise that if you leave here and Ramsay finds you then he'll make you tell him where we all are? And don't think that he wouldn't be able to find you, Paris, because the damn man has an uncanny knack of doing just that. Melanie said that she'd moved several times since the trial, but Ramsay still managed to find out her current address.'

'Maybe she's in the phone book,' Paris said flippantly.

He came away from the door in one stride and caught her shoulders to shake her 'Be serious, can't you? This isn't a game.'

It wasn't the first time he'd touched her since she'd been at the hotel, but it was the first time that he had been really close. She could feel the strength of his hands through her clothes, could breathe in his warmth and masculinity. It unnerved her, left her weak. She put up her hands to push him away but they only rested against his chest. She felt him grow still and lifted her eyes to look into his face.

It was impossible to hide her awareness of him—it was there in her wide, vulnerable gaze, in her softly parted mouth and trembling lower lip. Will made a low sound deep in his throat; his fingers tightened for a moment as his eyes, too, became intense. Paris thought that he was going to kiss her, was sure of it, and her heart almost stopped beating in anticipation. But he abruptly let her go and turned away, shoving his hands in his pockets.

'I'm sorry,' he said shortly. 'But you seem to be able to rile me as no one else can.'

He was silent for a moment, then turned to face her. His voice cool again, he said, 'Perhaps you don't take the situation as seriously as the rest of us because you've been away and weren't able to follow the story in the newspapers.

'As soon as it was realised that Ramsay was out for revenge, most of the people involved in the case clamoured for police protection. Everyone was afraid that they would be next. But there were so many of us that the police hadn't the resources to guard us all individually; that's why it was decided to bring us all here together. But they had to be careful, to make sure that Ramsay wasn't watching.'

He paused, picking his words, before saying, 'We were brought here in small groups, a few at a time, and it was a great relief when people got here safely. Eventually we were all here—except you. We all wondered where you were, what had happened to you. The police said that you were out of the country, but we weren't sure that they weren't just fobbing us off and that you too hadn't disappeared.'

'You asked them?' It wasn't really a question; she knew that he had.

'We all did.'

He was being evasive, but Paris looked at him with the light of discovery in her eyes. 'You do care.'

His mouth tightened. 'We've become a close community; we all care about each other. Which is why I insist on knowing why you want to leave here.'

So he came neatly back to the original question and avoided the main issue. Paris gave a small smile. 'I see. So you only want to know on everyone else's behalf?'

But he evaded that one too. 'So why?'

'I assure you that Ramsay won't find me and I won't be putting any of you in danger.'

'That isn't good enough.'

'It's all you're going to get.'

'I can ask Captain Waters.'

'Haven't you already?'

'Not yet, no, because . . .' He gave her an intent look, then said reluctantly, 'Is it because of this man you're involved with? Have you promised to go away with him or something?'

Again she had forgotten her imaginary lover, but Will obviously hadn't. 'Who told you I was involved with someone?'

He shrugged. 'Word got round. Well?'

'What if I am?' she temporised.

'You'd put yourself in danger just to be with him?'

'Maybe I care about him that much.'

A look of disgust came into Will's eyes. 'But he obviously doesn't care about you if he'd let you do it,' he said forcefully. 'No one who loved you would even contemplate it, let alone *urge* you to leave. What kind of man is he to suggest it?'

Paris looked at him for a moment, realising that he'd given away more than he intended, then shook her head. 'You're wrong; that isn't the reason.'

'You're not leaving to be with him?'

'No.'

'Is it because of your parents, your family?'

'Hardly. They don't need me.'

'It has to be a conference, then. Something to do with your job.'

She shook her head, walked to the door and reached for the knob.

But Will put his hand against the door, holding it shut. Angry now, he said, 'Damn you, Paris, stop making me play guessing games.'

'Just leave me alone, then. I'm not going to tell you and that's final.'

But he still held the door, and his voice grew harsh, his face set, as he said, 'Then I can think of only one other reason why you might want to leave.' Paris looked at him, her face wary, but didn't speak. 'It's because of me, isn't it?'

Her lashes came quickly down to hide her eyes, but not quickly enough; he saw that he was right 'But. . .' He said the word on a gasp of realisation and surprise.

Paris gave him a hefty push, caught him off balance so that he had to step back, wrenched the door open and ran.

CHAPTER SIX

Paris took refuge in the dining-room, losing herself in the queue of people waiting to serve themselves from the buffet, grateful for their noise and chatter. She was late in so it didn't take long to serve herself and go to find a seat next to Ben.

He smiled at her. 'Have you opened all your post?'

'Yes. I got a couple of presents from my parents.'

'Let's see. I bet your mother sent you something to wear and your father a book.'

Paris laughed. 'Is that what you always get?'

'Invariably. Was I right?'

'Close. But I think they must have colluded because my mother sent a chef's apron and oven gloves and my father a cookery book.'

'Can't you cook?'

She grimaced a little. 'Of course I can. I'm a whizz with a microwave. But they worry about me; they think I ought to settle down.'

'So, on the principle that the quickest way to a man's heart is through his stomach, they sent you the cookery gear.' Ben grinned. 'I think I'd like your parents; they seem to go for the direct, no-nonsense approach.'

Paris made a wry face. 'I suppose that is one way of saying that they have no subtlety.'

'And how about you—do you think it's time you settled down?'

Paris poured herself a glass of water. 'How did the carol rehearsal go?'

'Ouch!'

123

She raised her eyebrows as he winced. 'What's the matter?'

'I just bashed my head on your "Keep Off" sign.'

Smiling a little, Paris said, 'Does being ready to settle down depend upon age or circumstances?'

'Well, it is difficult to get married unless you meet someone you fall for, admittedly. But most men seem to reach an age when they feel that they've had enough of being on their own, that it's time to look around and choose someone to marry so that they can have a home and a family.' Ben gave her a sideways look. 'I suppose that sounds deadly boring to you, doesn't it?'

His words touched a raw spot so Paris hastily changed the subject by pushing her plate away and saying, 'Not boring—arrogant.'

'Arrogant?' He was astonished.

'The fact that men can think, because they've reached a certain point in their lives, that they can just go out and choose some girl to be their wife.'

'Ah, the feminist viewpoint.'

'Yes, exactly. Have there been girls in your past who've been really keen on you? Were they at an age when they were ready to settle down? What happened to them? Did you just say, "Well, thanks, but I'm not ready to commit myself yet."?'

'Something like that, yes,' Ben admitted. 'But it was a long time ago, when I was still training to be a barrister. I felt that I had to give that all my time and attention, which wouldn't have been fair on the girl. I would have been torn in two—my loyalties, my time divided—and probably would have failed in both my work and the relationship because of it. So I decided to concentrate on my career, get that under my belt first. Can't you identify with that?'

Paris had been looking at him rather belligerently, but now she slumped. Yes, she could identify with that kind of ambition. God, could she. She pushed the thought aside, afraid of dwelling on it, afraid of looking into her soul. Somehow the conversation had become apposite to her own life and she couldn't face it.

Ben gave a frown of admonishment. 'I have just realised that you have avoided my question yet again. Are you a woman of mystery, Paris?'

'Oh, definitely,' she said in relieved amusement. 'And you haven't told me how the carol rehearsal went.'

This time he accepted her change of subject and they got onto safer ground. After lunch they took part in a bridge competition which required so much concentration that Paris was mentally shattered afterwards. They didn't do too badly, though, and Ben told her that he was proud of his pupil.

Being cooped up in the card-room all afternoon, Paris had seen nothing of Will—or Melanie, come to that— but both of them were in the bar when she came down after changing for dinner and the party. Paris had put on black evening trousers with a black and gold tunic-top. Elegant but casual. Melanie was in a silver lamé sheath that was so close-fitting that she couldn't possibly have had any underwear on beneath it.

The other girl was the centre of a small crowd of sympathisers, all talking of the letter bomb, and nearly everyone who came into the bar went over to ask how she was. Will, though, wasn't among those around her. He was sitting on a stool at the other end of the bar counter, talking to some other men about cricket. When he saw Paris come into the room, he broke off the conversation and stepped over to her.

'Buy you a drink?'

She gave him a searching look but could read nothing in his face. Nodding, she said, 'OK. Thanks. A G and T, please.'

He gestured towards the stool he'd been using. Paris hesitated a moment then perched on it. The men he'd been talking to greeted her, but then moved aside a little, going on with their far more interesting views on the latest test match series in India.

'I didn't know you were a cricket buff,' she commented a minute later when he handed her a drink.

Will shrugged. 'One keeps up.' He leaned against the bar and took a swallow of his drink. 'How did you get on in the bridge tournament?'

'Fine. Ben's a good teacher.'

Paris glanced across at Melanie and the eyes of the two girls met momentarily. Paris gave her a sympathetic smile but only received a glare in return. Which was hardly surprising. Paris would have been angry herself if the man whom she was having an affair with invited an old flame to have a drink—and right in front of her eyes, too!

'I'd like to talk to you later,' Will was saying. He saw wariness come into her eyes and her face immediately close, so he said quickly, 'Nothing heavy. I just feel we need to talk, clear the air. I don't want you to feel that you have to get away from me.'

'I see.' She looked down at her drink.

'So will you?'

'Talk to you?' She raised her eyes to his, found him watching her intently. 'Perhaps.'

Will's mouth twisted a little. 'It's only to talk, not make a commitment.'

Paris took a drink, then said, 'Why aren't you with Melanie?'

'Why should I be with her?'

'Aren't you two an item?'

'No, we're not.' He said it with a definiteness that surprised her.

Her brows rose a little and she slid off the stool as she saw Ben and some other people stroll in. 'Maybe you ought to try telling Melanie that.' And she went over to join Ben and his friends.

The tension of their virtual imprisonment in the castle must have got on everyone's nerves, because they turned to the party that evening almost as a life-saver. Everyone had clubbed together to buy wine and beer, the hotel manager had donated a few bottles of Scotch, and one of the waiters turned out to be a virtuoso on the bagpipes. They danced reels, played silly party games, drank a little too much, and managed to forget where they were and why they were there.

It was midnight before they began to sing carols, and because they were still in a happy mood they started with the rousing ones, like 'Good King Wenceslas' and 'O, Come all ye Faithful'. Ben was playing his guitar so Paris stood against the wall, enjoying watching everyone letting their hair down, but definitely not singing.

She hadn't spoken to Will again that evening, although she'd seen him dancing and once they'd been in the same set for a Scottish reel. But their hands had touched as briefly as their eyes, and then they had gone back to their partners.

Paris had been dancing with Captain Waters at the time—he had been taking time off from his guardianship—and Will had been dancing with one of their fellow jurors, a middle-aged widow. Melanie too had joined in, but Paris hadn't seen her dancing with Will. So maybe what he had said was true.

But Paris had seen him go into the other girl's room with her own eyes, and could hardly think that their affair could have broken up so soon. And it was he who had rushed to Melanie's side when she had fainted earlier that day, although it already seemed ages ago.

Paris was sure that Will would never just ignore Melanie when they had been so close. Maybe it was Melanie, then? Had she got her eyes on someone else? But Paris could see no signs of it and, remembering the glare she'd got from the girl earlier, couldn't believe that it was Melanie's doing. So maybe something had happened between them.

A lot of wild reasons went through Paris's mind, but to conjecture was useless. And, after all, what did it matter? It would make no difference to Will's attitude to her. All right, he hadn't managed to conceal the fact that he still cared about her, but that was as far as it went—as far it would ever go.

He would never forgive her for what he thought she'd done; she knew that with absolute certainty. And there was little point in trying to tell him the truth because he wouldn't believe her and would only think worse of her for lying. But she was, anyway, to blame for losing the baby; it had been her responsibility. And there was no way that she could ever atone for it.

They were singing 'Silent Night' now, reducing everyone to misty-eyed pathos. Paris felt a touch on her arm and saw that Will had come up beside her.

'Our talk?'

She frowned. 'Now? Can't it wait till tomorrow?'

'I think it's best as soon as possible.'

Paris hesitated, then nodded. 'All right.'

Needing something to do with her hands, she picked up her glass and took it with her. They slipped out of the ballroom and walked down the carpeted corridor, found the television room empty and went inside.

She took only a few steps into the room and then turned to face him. 'So what do you want to say?'

'I was right this morning, wasn't I? The only reason you want to leave here is to get away from me.'

He didn't make it a question; he was already certain in his own mind, and Paris had little choice but to nod reluctantly. 'Yes.'

'I know I haven't made it exactly easy for you here, but I didn't think that—'

'It was already arranged before I came,' Paris broke in. She turned away from him. 'When the police came to collect me, I wouldn't go with them at first. I tried to make them take me somewhere else, some other safe house. But it was too near Christmas and they couldn't arrange it. The best they could promise was to find somewhere for me afterwards.'

Will was silent for a moment, then said tightly, 'You were so averse to seeing me again?'

She rounded on him indignantly. 'What else would you expect? We didn't exactly part on friendly terms. You threw me out! You said you were so disgusted that you couldn't bear to be near me. You—you looked at me as if I was dirt. Can you wonder that I didn't want to be cooped up in the same place as you for days, perhaps weeks on end?' Her voice broke and she took a hasty swallow of her drink.

'I wasn't exactly enthusiastic about coming here myself,' Will admitted. Then slowly, reluctantly, he added, 'Mostly, I suppose, because I'd never really got over you.'

She turned quickly to look at him at that, met his eyes for a brief instant and then looked hastily away again, her cheeks pale.

His voice became harsh as he burst out, 'I couldn't believe that you could go ahead and have an abortion. *And without even telling me.* The way I found out... I thought that was the worst part of it. But after you'd gone—that's when it really started to hurt.'

'I don't understand,' she said gropingly. 'You mean— because I wasn't there?'

'No. It was because I realised that I had been completely wrong about you—my thoughts, my hopes, my feelings—all of them wrong.'

He swung away from her, thumped his clenched fist against the back of a chair. Paris's hands tightened on her glass but she didn't speak, somehow knowing that what he would say next would be all-important to her.

Will gave a laugh of bitter self-mockery. 'For a start I thought that I meant more to you than your precious job.' She almost went to speak, then stopped, and was glad she had when he said forcefully, 'And don't tell me that I did, Paris, because I know darn well it isn't true. If you had loved me it would have been me you'd turned to when you were pregnant, not Emma. And if you'd loved me you would have wanted my child. OK, I know we weren't married, and that it was a mistake, but it was our child, for God's sake. Didn't that mean anything to you?' But then he answered his own question. 'But of course it didn't. I've asked myself that countless times, but it always comes back to the same thing. You were willing to destroy a life because it would have interfered with your ambition, with your career—'

'That isn't true,' Paris broke in, compelled to speak even though she knew it wouldn't make any difference.

Will looked as if he was going to argue, but then shrugged. 'So what is true?'

Her eyes widened and a wave of hope filled her. Might he believe her if she told him everything? But she couldn't just blurt it out, and there were things that needed to be brought out into the open first.

Paris paused for a moment, then said carefully, 'When I found out I was pregnant you were away. I needed someone—a woman—to talk to and Emma was the only friend I had who was that close. My mother—we're too distant; I could never have confided in her.

'It came as a shock to find I was pregnant when I thought that I couldn't possibly be. I wasn't prepared for it, for even the possibility of it, and I wasn't sure how *I* felt about it, let alone how you would feel. I needed to sort things out in my mind, to talk them through, but you weren't there. So I went to Emma. I know now that it was a terrible mistake, but it seemed right at the time. She was a lot older than me, so much more experienced.'

'I can guess what she said to you; you don't have to tell me,' he said curtly.

'Can you? I suppose you think she told me that I'd lose my job, that it would ruin my career.'

'Well, didn't she?'

'Yes, she did,' Paris admitted. 'But that was almost incidental. What she told me first and foremost was that if I went ahead with the pregnancy then I would lose you.'

Will's head came up as he stared at her.

'She kept on and on about it. She said that if you'd been ready to accept a child you would already have asked me to marry you, that you would always blame me for getting pregnant, for ruining your life. And that if we did marry because of the baby and we ever quarrelled you would always accuse me of trapping you into marriage. She said that you would grow to hate me for it.'

Will shook his head in angry disbelief. 'And you let her convince you of all that rubbish?'

'Yes, because there were a couple of things that ran very true.'

'And they were?'

She paused, licked lips that had gone dry. 'That you only asked me to move in with you because I couldn't afford to stay with her. And that you hadn't asked me to marry you.' She raised her eyes to meet his. 'You hadn't even said that you loved me. Not in so many words. Although I thought you did.'

He gazed at her for a moment, moved his lips as if he couldn't speak, then jerked out, 'Of course I loved you. I loved you almost from the first moment I met you.'

'You never said.'

'I thought you knew. That it was the same for you. I thought it went so deep that it didn't have to be said.'

'But it does. A woman has to be told, to be sure. And I wasn't sure of your feelings, only of my own. I didn't want to lose you. I would have done anything not to lose you—' She broke off, realising how wrong an impression those last words would make. It was impossible now to tell him that she hadn't had an abortion; he would never believe her.

Angry with herself, she went on, 'But those weren't my only reasons for not telling you. You'd made it pretty clear just what you thought of working mothers. Well, my views are completely the opposite: I think it's perfectly possible for a woman to have a family as well as a career. But I felt torn apart because you were so adamant about it. I was almost glad you were away because I had to make up my mind whether to give up a job that I loved and live by your rules, or whether it would be possible to work out some sort of compromise.'

'But instead you took what was for you the easy way out. You little coward.'

'You asked me to tell you the truth and I'm trying to explain. If you'll just listen—'

But Will said acidly, 'So that's your version of what happened, is it?'

There was such scorn in his voice that her heart sank. 'I've told you the truth.'

'Rubbish! You've told yourself it's the truth, convinced yourself of it. But nothing—not Emma, no one—

would have persuaded you to have an abortion if you hadn't wanted to—even if only subconsciously.'

She stared at him for a moment, then turned away, fighting a wave of terrible despair. In a few words he had exposed her own innermost fears—a dread that she had always been too afraid to face. It was true that she'd considered an abortion as a serious option, had thought about it for days, and, when she'd had the miscarriage, along with the sadness there had been an overwhelming feeling of relief.

Paris gripped the glass between her hands, held it so tightly that it shattered. What was left of the red wine inside it trickled over her fingers, red, like the blood of her gashed hand.

Without turning she said, 'Maybe you're right. I don't know. But it hardly matters now, does it?'

'Of course it damn well matters!'

She shook her head and walked forward to a table to set the broken glass down, her back still to him, blocking his view. She tried to press the vein in her palm but the blood was flowing freely now. 'No, it doesn't—because you don't trust me and you never will. You've convinced yourself of my guilt and nothing will change that So I really don't think there's any point in prolonging this discussion, do you?'

'You cold-hearted little bitch.'

She flinched but only said, 'Yes, of course. Whatever you say. Shut the door on your way out, won't you?'

She heard Will move, stride to the door, but then he paused. 'We haven't yet settled the question of your leaving here. There's no need for it.'

'You mean that you wouldn't bring up this subject again? You wouldn't throw it in my face every time we met?'

He drew in his breath, then said, 'No.'

Paris laughed unsteadily. 'Liar! You can't leave it alone. You admitted that yourself, the first time we talked.'

'I give you my word.'

Her hand was starting to hurt—a throbbing pain that made her grit her teeth so that she didn't answer.

'It would be stupid for you to go, Paris. Promise me you won't.'

'Just get out of here, Will.'

'Not until you promise.'

Her voice rose hysterically. 'All right! All right, I promise. Now get out of here and leave me alone!'

'My pleasure,' he said in curt anger, and went out, slamming the door behind him.

She slumped when he'd gone, the stubborn pride that had held her upright draining away. There was blood all over her clothes, and it would drip onto the owner's tartan carpet if she didn't get her hand bound up quickly.

The manager had a first-aid box in his office, but the office would probably be locked and he would be in the ballroom with all the others. And there was no way that she was going to go back there and let everyone see how stupid she'd been. There were some sticking plasters in her own room, but she wasn't sure that they would be enough to stop the bleeding.

She tried to think what to do but her silly head felt as if it was packed with cotton wool and she found it difficult to concentrate. I must have had too much to drink, she decided. Come on, pull yourself together.

With a rush of determination, Paris swung round to go to the door, but must have turned too quickly because her head began to spin, and she stumbled. Wow! Someone must have spiked her drinks for her to feel this light-headed.

She put her good hand on the back of a chair to support herself—the chair that Will had hit in frustrated anger. The poor chair was really going through it to-night. She made another effort but before she could take more than a faltering step the door opened and Will came back in.

'We forgot to arrange which of us would tell Captain Waters that you're staying. I'll do it, if you—' He broke off and took a stride towards her, frowning. 'Paris? Are you all right?'

He caught her as she swayed. She laughed. 'It would seem to be your role in life: to catch fainting females.'

'Yes, but— My God, your hand! What have you done? Oh, Paris, you little fool, *what have you done*?'

'I cut my hand on the glass.' She said the words quite clearly but they didn't seem to come out that way. Then she looked into Will's face, saw the horror there and understood. 'No! The glass broke and I cut myself, that's all!'

He put her in an armchair and looked at her searchingly, then picked up the broken glass and saw the blood on the table. Reassured, he took a clean handkerchief from his pocket and bound it round her hand. 'Hold it up, and wait here. I'll be right back.'

A great lethargy filled her and she felt overwhelmingly tired. Leaning back in the chair, Paris was glad to close her eyes. Her hand hurt, at one with the painful thoughts that chased each other through her brain. Will would never believe her, never forgive her; she had ruined her own life and, it seemed, his too. There was nothing she could do—nothing. A stupid tear trickled down her cheek.

He was back with the first-aid box and she hastily wiped her face, leaving a smear of blood.

Will took hold of her hand, opened her fingers and swore softly. 'Why the hell didn't you tell me, you little idiot?' He didn't seem to expect an answer but worked quickly on her hand, using some kind of antiseptic that stung and made her quickly turn away as she winced.

'I'm sorry to hurt you even more. Soon be over.'

So he thought her tears were from the pain of her hand. Well, that was all right. Let him think that.

When her hand was bandaged Will leaned back on his heels to look at her, picked up a clean swab and used it to wipe the smear of blood off her face. Then he gently stroked her cheek with the back of his fingers. 'You always were a proud, stubborn little fool. Never admitting that you were hurt, never letting me see you cry.'

At the rough tenderness in his voice, Paris came very close to letting him see just how much she was hurting. But the hurt was all inside and that was where it had to stay. She managed a smile. 'It was a stupid thing to do. Would *you* have wanted anyone to know?'

His eyes troubled, Will said, 'I meant what I said, Paris. I won't refer to—to what happened again. It's over. Forget it.'

She gave a laugh that was more a sigh of despair. 'Oh, Will. How can you ever forget a thing like that?'

He frowned. 'But surely you...?'

She shook her head tiredly. 'No. It's there all the time. All the time.' Leaning forward, she said, 'I'd like to go up to my room now.'

But Will didn't get up out of the way. Instead he stayed where he was, looking intently into her face. 'Have I been wrong about you, Paris? Have I?'

Now, if ever, was her opportunity to tell him the truth, but somehow there now seemed little point in it. In her own mind she was almost as guilty as she would have been if she'd had the termination.

She pushed herself to her feet and Will rose easily with her, stepped back to give her space. She didn't look at him as she walked to the door; she went to open it, then paused, and said with difficulty, 'I know that nothing will make any difference now, but I wasn't ready for motherhood. I wanted to keep my job. OK, maybe that was a selfish attitude, but have you thought that maybe yours was too? It just wasn't the right time, Will. Not for me and probably not for you either.'

'Would it ever have been the right time for us, then?' he said heavily.

Paris didn't answer. She went to open the door with her injured hand, changed to the other one, and went out of the room.

The party had broken up; there were just a few stragglers saying prolonged goodbyes round the door of the ballroom or waiting for the lift. Paris avoided them, running as swiftly up the stairs as she could manage and was out of breath by the time she'd reached her own landing.

She hadn't locked her door; the key had a large and heavy metal number-tag on it that was too big for a pocket or her evening purse so she usually didn't bother with it. Tonight she wished she had, because as soon as she switched on the light Paris realised that someone had been in her room. The drawers in the dressing table and the doors of the wardrobe were open and clothes scattered on the floor. Her duvet had been pulled back and the mattress soaked in some liquid that absolutely stank.

Moving nearer, Paris took a tentative sniff and realised that it was bleach. Yes, the empty container had been thrown down onto the carpet, leaving a white stain.

With a cry of anger, she picked up one of her good evening dresses and found that it had been savagely torn—hacked at with a pair of scissors from the look of it. Looking in the open drawers, she saw that her bottles of nail varnish and perfume had been emptied all over the contents. It didn't take much guessing to know who had done this. Melanie! Whatever had happened between her and Will, she had evidently blamed Paris for it and had taken her revenge in this petty, spiteful way.

After all that had happened today this could have been the last straw that threw Paris into the depths of despair but, strangely, all it did was make her seething mad. She had a good mind to go straight to Melanie and face her with it.

She half turned to march down to the other girl's room, but then stopped; Melanie would be expecting something like that and would make darn sure that her door was locked. And she would deny everything, of course; that's why she had come here at night to take her sneaky revenge. On Paris, of course; she wouldn't have dared do anything like this to Will. OK, so facing Melanie would have to wait. And in the meantime, what was she going to do about the room?

Paris decided to abandon it. The smell was so bad that she couldn't possibly have slept there anyway.

Rescuing for the morning some clothes that had escaped Melanie's tender attentions, she went down the corridor to the cleaner's storeroom. The elderly cleaner habitually left it unlocked; that was how Melanie had got hold of the bleach. On the wall was a chart on which the numbers of the occupied rooms were marked off. Paris picked one that was unoccupied, helped herself to bedlinen and towels, and went to find it.

Because it wasn't being used, the central heating in the room had been turned low, so that it felt cold and inhospitable. Paris turned up the thermostat, remembering how she'd done the same thing when she'd got home to her own flat from Budapest. That seemed a lifetime ago now, although it was less than a week.

She went to the windows to close the curtains but paused for a moment to look out. The moon was out,

silvering the snow, making it diamond-bright in the cold
frostiness of the night. The wind had blown away the
snow on the fir trees, so that they stood out like dark
sentinels, straight and stark, their branches no longer
bowed under the weight.

Soon they would be celebrating Christmas. And this
landscape was a far different one from that of
Bethlehem. There would not have been snow there, Paris
imagined; it would have been warm for the new baby,
the kings and the shepherds. Here the sheep would have
been taken down from the hills weeks ago and would
have a long wait for the grass to appear. And any
pregnant woman in this area would be afraid of the snow,
of being trapped in some highland croft and unable to
get help. But was that so very different from the Nativity?

Pulling the curtains closed, Paris got ready for bed as
quickly as she could with her bandaged hand, got in and
pulled the duvet close around her for warmth.

Because she was cold it took a while for her to go to
sleep, her thoughts drifting always back to that so-called
talk with Will. It had been more of a full-scale fight,
but she was strangely glad that it had taken place. And
relieved too. At least she had faced her guilt—that terrible cancer that had been eating away at her soul—and
in admitting the basic cause had found an inner peace.
Nothing would make up for the miscarriage, of course,
but she felt better able to live with it now.

She fell asleep at last but woke in the middle of the
night. It wasn't from a bad dream or anything; she woke
with a smile of realisation because the way to atone had
come to her at last. And it was really so simple, so very
simple. She smiled again, turned over and went back to
sleep.

It was almost ten o'clock the next morning when Paris
found that she had unknowingly created a crisis. The

cleaner, thinking her at breakfast, had gone to her room and found the terrible state it was in, so had immediately called the manager. He had tried to find Paris and, when he couldn't, had in turn called Captain Waters. He and his police colleague were both in the room when she strolled in there to see what she could do about her clothes.

'Good morning. It's quite a mess, isn't it?'

They both swung round to stare at her. Captain Waters gave a sigh of relief. 'Are you all right? We'd started to worry about you.'

Paris put her injured hand, covered now with just a large sticking plaster, in her pocket. 'Yes, fine.'

'You'd better go and tell everyone to call off the search,' he said to the policeman. When he'd gone he said, 'How did this happen?' and gestured at the room.

'I don't know. I found it like this when I came up last night, so I slept in an empty room because of the smell.'

He gave her a shrewd look. 'Are you sure you have no idea who did it?'

'None,' she said blandly.

He looked as if he didn't believe her and was going to say so, but just then Will strode into the room.

Coming straight to Paris, he took hold of her arm in a firm grip. 'Where the hell have you been?' he demanded brusquely.

There was anger in his voice but it was the anger of relief, and she recognised it for what it was, what it meant, and her heart leaped.

'Er—if you'll excuse me for a moment.' Captain Waters went out, closing the door behind him.

'I thought you'd got lost again,' Will said curtly.

'Again?'

'When you didn't arrive here with the rest of us, and I thought Ramsay had got to you,' he explained. His eyes met hers, wry, rueful. 'It was hell then, waiting, wondering. The thoughts that kept going through my mind... And then to have it happen again this morning.'

She lifted a hand to touch his face gently. 'Will you do something for me?'

'What?'

'Will you kiss me?'

He froze, then raised a cynical eyebrow. 'For old times' sake?'

'No.' She shook her head. 'For now. For the me I am now.'

For a long moment Will didn't move and she thought that he was going to deny her, but his grip tightened on her arm and he drew her slowly towards him, his eyes holding hers. She could feel the tension in his hand, see it in his face. He lowered his head to hers, touched her lips with his mouth. For an instant it was as if time had stood still and he was kissing her for the very first time all over again. And yet it was so achingly familiar too— the searing heat of his lips, their firmness. But his lips had never quivered like this before, never been so hungry and yet so afraid.

Her mouth opened under his, soft and yielding. She felt his swift intake of breath, the undeniable tremor of emotion that ran through him. Desire suffused her like a burning ache deep in her body, but her overpowering emotion was one of excitement. It was possible—that resolve she had taken in the middle of the night. Now that he had kissed her it was surely possible.

His kiss deepened and Paris lifted her hand to his shoulder. But she brushed his neck as she did so, and it was as if her touch brought him back to reality, because Will suddenly let her go, stepping abruptly away. He stared at her, the hunger and need plain in his face but being subjugated to an even greater need to control his feelings.

'Paris, it's no good; I—'

But she held up a hand to silence him. 'It was only a kiss,' she said lightly, then walked to the door. 'I think I can hear someone outside.'

On opening it, she saw Mrs Paston and a couple of other women, come to see the wreckage of her room. Will slipped away while they were still exclaiming with horror. The women immediately began to help her to sort through her clothes, rescuing what could be washed and putting into a depressingly growing pile the number of things that were completely ruined.

'We all know who did this,' Mrs Paston said grimly. 'And she ought to be punished in some way. At the least she should be made to pay compensation for all this.'

'Nothing can be proved,' Paris pointed out. 'And I suppose it's my fault for not locking my door.'

She decided to keep to her new room and took the rest of her things along, then went down to the manager's office to get the key. He was on the phone, using the only line in the place that was connected to the outside world. Paris made signs for a key and he gestured to a board on the wall behind him.

Number 315, the one she wanted, was easy to find, but she noticed another key nearby with a plastic tag reading, 'Spare passkey. All floors.' With a small sigh of exhilaration Paris lifted that down as well and slipped it into her pocket.

After the party last night, most of the adults wanted to have a restful day, although some games were organised for the children. Everyone had heard of the attack on Paris's room and she was inundated with offers to lend her clothes, some of which she was glad to accept, although they weren't always the kind of thing that she would have chosen herself. But they were offered out of kindness and her acceptance was grateful, pleasing the donors.

Her delicate silk underclothes and night things had been one of Melanie's prime targets and had been entirely ruined, so that night Paris had to wear a borrowed nightdress. She waited until gone midnight, then put on a pair of lightweight mules that hadn't been damaged, and slipped a borrowed dressing-gown, long and dark-coloured, over her nightdress. This time she remembered to lock her door, putting the heavy key in her pocket along with the passkey.

The corridor outside her room was lit only by two dimmed wall-lights—one at the head of the stairs, the other by the lift—but they were enough to see her way by. Because she'd changed her room, Paris had further to go to reach the stairs. She walked quietly along, letting the excitement and anticipation take hold, praying that it would all go right, this great adventure she was about to set out on.

There was a soft whirr and the doors of the lift suddenly opened. Paris quickly ducked into a doorway, afraid of being seen. Whoever it was who came out must have been alone; there was no sound of voices and the person was very quiet.

Peeping out, Paris saw a woman walk along and stop at the turret stair where Paris had followed the wet footprints. When she reached it the woman glanced back and Paris saw that it was Melanie. Surely she wasn't going to have another go at her room? Paris thought indignantly. But Melanie went up the stair, lighting her way with a torch.

Paris hesitated; she had important business of her own tonight, but curiosity overcame her and she went quickly to the staircase. The cold air from outside made her pull the dressing gown closer around her, and again she hesitated, but then went up the stairs. The wooden door at the top was ajar and she quietly pushed it further open, trying to see outside. But the angle prevented her so she pushed it wide and stepped cautiously out onto the roof.

The sky was black tonight, with dark clouds obscuring the moon, and it was very cold and windy. There was no sign of Melanie, although a chimney-stack blocked her view of all the parapet.

Paris felt for the anorak but it wasn't there. She took another step forward to peer past the chimneys. There was a sudden noise from behind and above her, but before she could turn something hit her in the middle of the back and sent her flying towards the edge of the roof.

She felt herself falling but managed to twist sideways as she did so, avoiding the battlemented edge so that she ended up on the roof instead of overbalancing and pitching down to the ground so far below. She had fallen heavily and for a moment lay stunned, as much by fright as lack of breath. But then she realised that Melanie must have pushed her and got indignantly to her feet, having had about enough, prepared to do battle.

Groping her way to the door, Paris found the handle and turned it. Nothing happened. She turned it again and pushed against the door, but still it didn't move. With utter disbelief she realised that it was locked. Melanie had deliberately left her out here alone in the freezing cold.

CHAPTER SEVEN

'MELANIE! This isn't funny,' Paris yelled, banging her fist against the wood of the door. 'Come and unlock this door at once.'

She leaned her left ear against the panels, straining to hear, covering her other ear to try and cut out the noise of the wind that howled around the tower. But she could hear nothing, so banged on the door again.

'OK, you've had your fun; now let me in.' Nothing happened although she waited for several minutes. Paris shoved her hands into her pockets, already shivering with cold, then placed her mouth close to the door and shouted, 'You want me to apologise to you? All right, then—I'm sorry I followed you up here. Now, please, Melanie, let me in. It's really cold out here.'

She was angry at having to apologise, annoyed that she had to plead, but her teeth were chattering and the doorway gave little protection from the wind. The air was so cold that she might as well not have been wearing any clothes at all, they had so little warmth in them.

'Please, Melanie. I'm really sorry. *Please* open the door.' She could hear the begging note in her voice and despised herself for it, but was still confident that Melanie was standing on the other side of the door, hugely enjoying the silly prank she'd pulled, and would soon open it to see Paris's discomfiture for herself.

It was only when Melanie still didn't open it and let her back into the warmth that it dawned on Paris that maybe this wasn't just another vengeful trick, that maybe Melanie wasn't going to open the door at all and had left her out on the roof to freeze to death. But Paris wasn't about to be left out there to die tamely, so she decided she'd better do something about it.

The most obvious thing was to go along the parapet to the next turret and see if the door there was unlocked. It took a lot of courage to leave the comparative shelter of the doorway and go along the roof edge in the fierce wind.

The snow, which had melted a little and then frozen again several times, was treacherous under her slippered feet, and the wind constantly buffeted her, threatening to knock her off balance and make her slip over. Twice she almost fell, and with a curse realised that the only way she was going to get safely across was on her hands and knees. Anger kept her going along the long length of the building and when she reached the other turret at last she found, without surprise, that that door, too, was locked.

Paris leaned against it, her breath tight in her chest, her teeth chattering so loudly that she could hear nothing else. It was then that she screamed, knowing that she couldn't fight the cold much longer.

Across the courtyard she could make out a light in the gatehouse where the police guards were, but it might just as easily have been miles away, because the wind took her voice and made it just a shrill pipe in the howling cacophony. Paris screamed again, becoming really frightened now, but then huddled in the doorway and tried not to panic, tried to think, to find some way out of this.

Working out the plan of the hotel, she realised that this must be the turret where Ben had his suite, that he must be asleep in the bedroom only a few yards away from her. Leaning over the parapet as far as she dared, she yelled his name over and over again, but no light came on to shine in the windows, he didn't look out to see who called him.

She leaned back in the doorway again, knowing that she couldn't last out much longer. Pressing herself against it, willing the door to open, she felt something press into her hip and realised that it was her doorkey with the heavy metal tag.

Feverishly she took it out of her pocket and tried it in the lock; then, when that didn't work, she tried the passkey, but both were made for small Yale locks, not the locks on these heavy doors. She slumped again, hope gone. Her room key was freezing cold to her fingers, making them burn with the cold, and she almost dropped it. Then she had a sudden idea.

Going to the very end of the parapet, she leaned out as far as she could, gripping the last merlon with her left arm and swinging her right backwards and forwards; trying to take careful aim in the dark, trying to get as much impetus as she could. Then she hurled the heavy key at the nearest window with all the strength she had left.

She heard it smash even above the noise of the wind, the glass shattering. She waited breathlessly, petrified that Ben might have slept through it. But then light glimmered between the cracks in the curtains, they were pulled back and she could see Ben's silhouette against the light.

'Ben!' She screamed out his name with all the strength she had left. 'Ben, up here. Help me.'

He glanced up and the next second he was gone, but it seemed an age before the door behind her opened and he was helping her inside, exclaiming, asking questions. But she couldn't answer, could only cry with relief and cold.

Ben was magnificent; he carried her to his room, put her into his beautifully warm bed and gave her a slug of his whisky, before picking up the phone. Within minutes Captain Waters was there and then she found herself standing under a hot shower, nightdress and all, supported by both men who were getting as wet as she was.

Very gradually the terrible shivering eased and finally stopped as warmth crept back into her veins. Then they gave her towels and let her dry herself before she put on a pair of Ben's pyjamas. There was hot coffee waiting, strongly laced with whisky, which she drank gratefully as she again sat in Ben's bed, the duvet held close around her, while they each massaged one of her feet.

'Can you feel this?' Captain Waters asked.

'Yes, a little.'

'Good, hopefully you won't get frostbite, then. Now, would you like to tell us what you were doing out there in this weather and at this time of night?'

'She locked me out there.'

They exchanged glances. 'She?'

'M-Melanie.' Paris shivered again as she remembered.

'Oh, hell!' Captain Waters said feelingly. 'When she got that letter bomb I thought she was in the clear. What happened?'

'I saw her going up to the roof again and—'

'What do you mean "again"? Had you seen her go up there before?'

Paris nodded, then took another drink so that she could go on. 'Yes. I saw her a few nights ago. At least, I was pretty sure it was her.'

'Why didn't you tell me?' he said sharply.

'I wasn't absolutely sure. But I was going to tell you, but the next morning the bomb came, so—so I didn't,' she finished lamely.

'You were taken in as we all were,' he said ruefully. 'Sorry. Go on, please.'

'I didn't think she'd seen me tonight, but she must have done. When I followed her she was hiding behind the door. She pushed me out onto the roof and I fell down. Then she went back in and locked the door. I— I thought it was just revenge, the same reason for her making a shambles of my room, ruining my clothes. I kept banging on the door, expecting her to open it, but— but she left me out there. I yelled but no one heard because of the wind. And she'd taken the coat, so—'

'What coat?'

'The first time I went out on the roof, to have a look, there was a coat outside, by the turret. A thick anorak. I thought one of your men must have left it there.'

Captain Waters grimaced, stood up. 'Can you manage both feet for a while?' he said to Ben. 'I think I'd better go and make a few phone calls.'

When he'd gone, Paris said, 'Have I been abysmally stupid?'

'You and the rest of us too, by the sound of it. Have some more whisky.' He poured them both a generous helping. 'By the way, what were you doing out in the corridor anyway? Or needn't I ask?' Paris flushed a little and he said, 'I see that I needn't.' He began rubbing her feet again. 'Can you feel your toes yet?'

'Yes, but I'm quite enjoying having them rubbed.'

He laughed and went on for a while, but then found her his thickest pair of woollen socks to put on. They were bright red. 'A trendy aunt gave them to me for Christmas,' he explained. 'I was going to forget to take them home with me when we leave here.'

Captain Waters came back and pulled up a chair to sit beside her. He looked grim. 'I'd better come clean,' he said to them. 'We've been a bit suspicious of Melanie Truscott all along because she had some contact with Ramsay while he was in prison. However, we decided to let her come here with all of you but to keep a close eye on her until we were sure of her, one way or another. She seemed to take a fancy to your ex-boyfriend so we let him in on it and persuaded him to watch her for us.'

Paris stared. 'Will? You mean he wasn't keen on her himself?'

The captain shook his head. 'No. And at first he was very reluctant to help us. It took some persuasion to make him agree.'

'I suppose by "persuasion" you mean coercion,' she said shortly.

He grinned. 'I'm afraid so. He cut up rough until we promised him that we'd do everything in our power to get *you* here as soon as we possibly could.'

'Oh.' Paris could find nothing else to say.

'He kept his word, much against his will, but once the letter bomb arrived and we thought she was in the clear I'm afraid he dropped her like the proverbial hot cake.'

Paris, remembering Will being drawn into Melanie's room, was wondering just how close a watch on her they had considered it necessary for him to keep. She frowned. 'But I don't understand. Are you saying that you're now suspicious of Melanie again?'

'What reason could she possibly have for going out on the roof, unless she was sending Ramsay some kind of signal?'

'But the letter bomb? She didn't fake her shock at getting that. I swear it was genuine.'

'Yes, I'm sure it was. But what if Ramsay deliberately sent it to her to divert suspicion from her?'

'Without telling her, you mean?'

'Yes.'

They both looked at him with troubled eyes. 'But how would she signal to him?' Ben objected. 'With a torch or something?'

'No, much more simple than that. With a portable phone, of course. We went through her luggage when she arrived, the same way we went through everyone else's, but phones are so small nowadays, she might have been able to conceal it. We didn't body-search everyone. Her difficulty, though, is that we're surrounded by hills; portables don't work well here; that's one of the reasons why we chose the place. But they might up on the roof.'

'So you think Ramsay probably knows where we are?' Ben said slowly.

'I'm afraid I do, yes.'

'What will you do—move us somewhere else?'

Captain Waters shook his head. 'No, this has gone on long enough. I've spoken to my superiors and we've decided to try and trap him. But we'll need your help—both of you,' he said, looking at them intently.

'Of course,' Ben said at once.

But Paris looked at the captain warily. 'What sort of help?'

'Nothing very onerous. I want Melanie to think you're still out there on the roof, frozen stiff.'

'Oh, nice.'

'It's all right, you don't have to go out there again,' he said quickly, seeing the sudden alarm in her face. 'You can stay hidden here in Ben's suite. He can have breakfast served here, but he'll have to put in an appearance downstairs during the day, to allay any suspicion.'

'What about the cleaner, and the broken window?' Ben pointed out.

'That will be taken care of. No problem.'

'But surely I'll be missed,' Paris objected.

'Yes, but the police and I will naturally want to keep that quiet so as not to alarm everyone. But we'll look just worried enough for anyone who's watching us to notice.'

'You mean Melanie.'

'Of course.'

'But what's the point?'

'You following Melanie out onto the roof tonight must have stopped her from sending a message. Maybe she'll try again tomorrow night—and we'll be listening.'

'Can you do that?' Ben asked.

'Oh, yes, quite easily.'

Paris said, 'But other people might miss me, too.'

They both knew that she meant Will, but the captain said, 'We'll say that you've got a bad cold and are spending the day in bed.'

'Which will probably be true by tomorrow,' Paris said pessimistically. 'If Melanie notices that you're anxious and I'm not around, then Will might notice as well. Could you tell him that I'm all right?'

'No.'

'Why not?'

'Same reason as Ramsay didn't tell Melanie about the letter bomb: like hers, Will's reaction has got to be authentic.'

'But surely if you were searching everywhere for me you'd be bound to go out on the roof and look?'

'We'd have no reason to. And we'd be concentrating our search outside, questioning the tradesmen, looking in their vans, thinking that you'd run away on your own initiative. Now wouldn't we?'

Paris was silent, realising that he'd got it all worked out. She nodded, suddenly tired. 'All right; if there's no other way.'

Leaning back against the pillows, she fell instantly into a deep sleep and was unaware of Ben sitting in a chair beside her, watching over her, or of a policeman quietly replacing the broken window and clearing up the glass.

She woke late and found Ben still sitting patiently beside her, waiting to send for his breakfast. Some clothes had been brought from her room and by the time she'd dressed in the bathroom the food had arrived. Paris ate ravenously; she'd never felt so hungry in her life and food had never tasted so good. Even the thick porridge, which she usually avoided, tasted like manna from heaven this morning.

Ben watched her in grinning admiration. 'I pity the poor man who ever takes you on a skiing holiday,' he remarked.

She made a face at him and he laughed as he stood up, his own meal finished.

'I'd better go downstairs and look innocent as I mingle.'

'Do you have anything I can read? I shall be bored just watching television all day.'

'I've some law books; some of the cases make quite interesting reading.'

'Don't you have any novels or magazines?'

'No, but I'll try and bring you some up.'

'Oh, thanks. I like *Vogue* and *Cosmopolitan*—that kind of thing.'

'Sorry, but those are definitely out. If anyone saw me bringing that type of magazine up here they might get the wrong idea about me.'

Paris laughed richly. 'OK, just a book will do, then.'

When Ben had gone, she felt a strange mixture of emotions. For a start she felt lonely and out of place. Having to stay in Ben's suite was like visiting people you didn't know very well and being left to amuse yourself in a strange house. Only, this sitting-room, of course, was far more restricting.

She could see that outside it was snowing heavily again, which made her feel even more shut in. The door was locked and she had been warned not on any account to use or answer the phone, making the room like a prison, within a citadel that was no longer safe.

Because of Melanie's treachery and Ramsay's knowledge of their whereabouts, Paris should have felt afraid, but strangely she didn't. Instead, being still alive after coming safely through last night, she felt oddly elated, almost as if fate had forgiven her and allowed her to start again.

In her imagination she saw it almost as a sign that the way which she had decided on had been approved and she was going to be allowed to carry it through. Not that she'd been able to last night. But there was tonight. And today was Christmas Eve, she remembered with a smile of satisfaction.

It was a couple of hours before Ben came back. He'd brought her a paperback from the hotel's library and yesterday's paper, but it was the news of what was happening downstairs not of the outside world that she really wanted to hear.

'Well, there's no panic or anything,' Ben told her. 'Captain Waters is playing it down, and nobody knows that you're missing.'

'Has—er—anyone asked for me?'

Ben grinned. 'I suppose by "anyone" you mean Will Brydon?' He shook his head. 'Not that I know of, but it's still early yet; for all anyone knows you could be sleeping late.'

He stayed with her till lunchtime, then went downstairs again, while Paris had to make do with soup and sandwiches that were smuggled up to her on the cleaner's trolley.

In the afternoon she read and watched television, whiling the hours away until Ben came again about five-thirty. Twice the phone had rung, and the first time she had automatically reached out to answer it, but had managed to stop herself in time.

Was it Melanie checking to make sure that she wasn't there? Paris wondered with a shiver. Just making certain she was lying up on the roof, dead and frozen? The thought brought the nightmare back again and she had to go and huddle against the radiator, so intense was the memory of the cold.

When Ben came she told him about the phone calls and he reported them to Captain Waters. Ben listened for a while as the captain talked to him, then said goodbye and put the phone down. Turning to her, he said, 'It seems there have been several calls to your room too. Will called you—twice, late in the morning—then went up there and banged on the door. When he didn't get any reply he went to see Mike Waters.'

'And?' Paris said impatiently.

'It seems you'd talked about leaving and he was afraid the police had spirited you away.'

'So what did Captain Waters tell him?' she asked, intensely interested now.

'Our good captain wouldn't commit himself either way. Which made Brydon somewhat angry evidently. He informed Mike Waters that if anything happened to you he would hold him personally responsible for it. He also demanded to be allowed to speak to you on the phone, and wasn't at all pleased when Mike refused.' He laughed. 'Mike says his desk won't ever be the same again after the fist-bashing it got.'

'Really?' She grinned widely, inordinately pleased.

Ben walked over to the spiral stair leading to the bedroom above. 'I'm going to change for dinner. It's special tonight. Venison soup and salmon fillets *en croûte*, and a whole range of puddings and cheeses to follow. I think they're going to do you proud too.'

'You mean they're sending some up for me?'

He gave her a sardonic grin. 'Not quite. You're having a ham sandwich instead of cheese.' Then he ran up the stairs as she indignantly threw a cushion at him.

* * *

It was Captain Waters himself who brought her food that evening and stayed with her while she ate.

'Melanie is safely downstairs in the dining-room,' he told her. 'She's being watched and if she makes a move I'll be informed.'

He had brought her a large tray and she was pleased to see that she was sharing the meal being served downstairs, and he had even brought her a bottle of wine.

'We searched her room today,' he added. 'We were right: she has got a portable phone—a very small one that she must have concealed on herself when she arrived.' Neither of them said anything but Paris's mind immediately went to Melanie's ample bosom, wondering if the phone had been concealed in her bra. 'It's quite likely that she'll try and make contact with Ramsay again tonight, and if she does we'll be waiting.'

'Won't she expect to see me up there?' she asked.

Captain Waters grinned. 'Yes, so we've made up a very lifelike—or perhaps I should say death-like—dummy which is now under several inches of fallen snow. Don't worry; her just going out onto the roof will be evidence enough, but we're hoping to listen in on her conversation with Ramsay so that we can get him in our net.'

'It will probably be late before she goes up there,' Paris observed. 'She'll have to wait until everybody goes to bed, won't she?'

'Probably. If you like, I'll let you know when she goes out there. Ben can answer the phone, just in case it's anyone else.'

'Thanks.'

He stood up to go, then held a key out to her. 'You may need this. We found it in the pocket of your dressing gown when we dressed the dummy in it last night.'

Paris took the passkey, blushed a little as she again said, 'Thanks.'

* * *

She had expected it to be really late before Ben came up to the suite, but he came in around midnight, saying that they had broken up early because of the children, who were excited because it was Christmas Eve. Their parents had been afraid that they either wouldn't get to sleep at all or would wake them at some unearthly hour in the morning to open the presents that a dozen 'Father Christmases' were covertly loading into stockings.

Ben had nothing much to report, but sat companionably with her as they finished off her bottle of wine. As the time passed they grew tense, waiting, both of them wondering if Melanie had changed her mind and hadn't gone up to the roof at all. But at one o'clock the phone rang and Ben answered it. He spoke only briefly, then put the receiver down and turned to Paris. 'They've got her. And they were able to listen. She was definitely talking to Ramsay.'

Paris went to ask him if Ramsay was nearby but stopped; she didn't want to feel any fear, not tonight.

'Well, I'm going to bed. Goodnight, Paris.'

'Goodnight.'

He went up the stairs, closing the door behind him, and ten minutes later Paris was out of the room and running lightly down the stairs, the passkey clutched in her hand. There was no one about; the whole hotel was asleep, waiting for Christmas Day. There was no one to see her in a borrowed nightdress, her hair loose, a light of eager anticipation in her green eyes.

The key turned easily in the lock of Will's door and she gave a small sigh of relief as she turned the handle and slipped inside. The room was in darkness but she made out the layout in the soft light from the corridor. It was a large room with a heavily carved four-poster bed dominating the centre. Paris didn't take any notice of anything else. She saw Will's sleeping figure and gently closed the door.

It made quite a loud click as the lock shot home, and Will stirred. She couldn't see him, but she heard the change in his breathing and guessed that he was awake. Walking quietly on the soft carpet, her feet bare, Paris moved towards the bed.

There was a flurry of movement as Will turned over, and then came his voice, sharp and forceful. 'Get out of here, Melanie. I've already told you I'm not interested.'

Reaching the bed, Paris pulled back the covers and slid into it, encountering Will's hand as he reached for the bedside lamp.

'Damn it, Melanie, don't you listen? Get out of here before I darn well throw you out.'

'Well, if you really want me to go. . .' Paris murmured softly.

He was sitting up and had put one hand on her arm, was reaching past her for the light with the other. But when she spoke he immediately grew still. 'Dear God,' he said in little more than a whisper. 'Paris?'

She found his face with her hand and leaned forward to lightly kiss him on the mouth. 'Now do you know me?'

He didn't return the kiss, but went on with his original movement, found the light switch and turned on the lamp. Paris was disappointed but didn't let it show, instead smiling at him with imps of mischief dancing in her eyes.

She hadn't expected him to be angry, hadn't expected him to say harshly, 'Are you playing some kind of game, Paris? Disappearing and reappearing. I thought you'd broken your promise and got the police to take you somewhere else. Captain Waters as good as admitted that you'd gone.'

'No, I was here all the time. But it's a long story. Why don't I tell you about it later?' And she again leaned forward and would have kissed him, but he stopped her.

'Tell me now.'

'No, later.' She lifted her hands to the buttons of his pyjamas and began to undo them.

He caught her wrist, his eyes probing her face. 'Why are you here?'

'I came to give you your Christmas present,' she said lightly, and slipped her free hand inside his jacket. Finding his nipple, she caressed it gently.

Will stiffened, but said, 'And what makes you think I want you in my bed?'

Paris raised her brows. 'You don't? OK, we'll do it on the floor. I seem to remember we've had some pretty good times on the floor.' She kissed his throat. 'On the ground.' Her mouth moved to his ear. 'And in the car.' She bit gently. 'In that cave on the beach.' She traced his jawline and her tongue touched his lips, delicately tantalising. 'Then there was the hay barn out in the countryside when we got caught in that terrible thunderstorm. Now that was *really* something.'

'Are you trying to seduce me?' His voice had changed, sounded odd.

'You got it.' She freed her hand and carried on with the buttons. This time he didn't stop her, but when she raised her eyes to glance at him Paris found him watching her, a strangely rueful look in his eyes.

'Where did you get that terrible nightdress?'

She glanced down at the all-enveloping gown with its high neck and long sleeves, which was a dozen sizes too large for her. 'Mrs Paston lent it to me.'

'My God, no wonder the judge looks so frustrated.'

She smiled. 'You don't like it? I can always take it off.'

Heart beating, she waited. For a long moment Will didn't speak, then he said harshly, 'Are you protected, Paris?'

She had known that he would ask, was expecting it and had her answer ready. 'I don't make the same mistake twice.'

Grim lines showed round his mouth. 'That's what I thought. I don't know that I want this.'

'Why kick a gift-horse in the teeth?' she said pertly, and was pleased to see him smile despite himself.

Putting her hands on his chest, she let them rise caressingly to his shoulders, pushed off his jacket and drew it down his arms. Then she bent to kiss his nipples. He quivered, tried to control it, but couldn't. 'So do I take it off?' she breathed softly.

'No.' Her heart froze for agonisingly long seconds, until Will said, his voice thick, 'I'll take it off.'

He did so slowly, revealing to his gaze first her long, shapely legs, then the tempting loveliness of her slender body: the roundness of her breasts, the dark shadow of her thighs, the slimness of her waist—beauty concealed beneath prim and proper white flannel.

Will caught his breath, his eyes drinking her in. So a Victorian bridegroom must have felt when he saw his bride naked for the first time on their wedding night. 'God, I'd almost forgotten how lovely you are,' he murmured.

Lifting his hand, he let his fingertips touch her breast, so lightly, like the caress of a butterfly's wings. And yet it sent a great tremor of awareness running through her. Paris didn't try to hide it; there would have been no point—they both knew that she'd never been able to resist him. And anyway, she wanted him to know that she needed him—needed him desperately.

Pushing him gently back down on the pillow, Paris knelt over him as she drew back the duvet and tossed it aside. He was wearing pyjama trousers too, which made her smile. When they'd been together they had never worn anything in bed. But that had been a long, long time ago.

Undoing the button at his waist, she slowly pulled them down his legs, letting her nails run along his skin as she did so. Will made a hoarse sound deep in his throat, and again when she moved over him and let her hair trail across his broad chest.

Lowering herself a little until she was almost touching him, she let her nipple find his and rubbed herself teasingly against him. He groaned as his tiny nipple hardened and she felt the heat of anticipation on his skin. Her own breathing quickened and she felt her own breasts swell in awakened desire.

Will gripped her arms and she knew that he would soon become too excited and would take over, but she didn't want that—not yet. So Paris moved off him and knelt beside him, letting her fingers explore him instead. In the years since they had parted she had so often imagined herself in just this position, had thought that she knew every inch of his body, but seeing him naked now was an intense delight that no memory could compete with.

It was the contrasts in him that she saw anew: his whipcord muscles under the softness of his skin, the firmness of his features against the delicacy of his lashes, the strength in his hands and yet the gentleness of his touch. His broad chest was so powerful but his nipples so sensitive, his aroused manhood so hard and yet he trembled when she touched him there.

And yet in some ways it was almost as if time had stood still. She didn't have to try and remember what pleased him: her hands moved of their own accord, instinctively finding the places that made him catch his breath, that would make him groan if she stayed there.

But she teased him, making him sweat but then moving on somewhere else until he grew tense again—playing with him, driving him mad with desire.

Then she bent and let her lips and tongue add to the game, circling his nipples, gently tugging at his ear, caressing him intimately until he groaned aloud and his hand found her shoulder, gripping it as tremor after tremor ran through him.

But then she was gone again, to trail her tongue along his arm, tasting the salt of his sweat, nuzzling his neck, feeling the tension in it, hearing his heart thudding in his chest, her senses full of the arrant masculinity of him. His body was trembling with almost uncontrollable need, was tense now, ready for love. She let her fingers brush his manhood again, lightly caress the heart of him, until he cried out and suddenly surged up and over her, unable to bear it any longer.

Will was so excited that he made no attempt to arouse her, instead taking her with a primitive hunger that wasn't to be denied. Fierce, almost savage hunger. But his need for her was more than enough for her to open to him willingly, to hold him tightly, exultantly inside her as he thrust with all his strength.

Her body rose to meet him, fuelling the flame of his passion, lifting them both to the heights of sexual ecstasy. Will cried out, then gasped out her name on a long groan that obliterated the long, empty years, the hurt and the mistrust. Her own moans joined his and she found that she was crying with happiness.

He seemed to be over her, holding her, taking her for ever, but then the shudders that ran through him slowly faded and his body relaxed. He lay down but still held her closely in his arms and, when his breathing had eased a little, drew her to him and kissed her.

'You're crying.' Putting up his hand, he clumsily wiped her tears.

'I know.' She laughed huskily. 'And so are you. Oh, *Will.*'

'I've wanted this so much, so much.' His voice was full of the remembered longing, but then grew rueful as he said, 'When I thought of you with your new lover, it nearly drove me crazy with jealousy. Although I had no right, I know, but—'

'There isn't anyone else,' she interrupted. 'I made him up. I'm sorry, but you were so antagonistic towards me when I arrived here that I felt I needed some kind of protection from you.' She put her hand against his chest. 'I thought you still hated me, you see.'

Will frowned, hesitated. 'I did. I convinced myself that I did. But when I saw you, looking lovelier than ever, all the old longing came back. I was angry, I'd hoped I was over you, so I took it out on you. But all the time— all the time—I was wanting this. Even though I told myself a thousand times that it was the last thing I wanted.'

Paris chuckled and kissed his chin. 'Well, it's a good job one of us did something about it, or I think we'd both have died of frustration.'

He smiled and cupped her breast possessively. 'It's the best Christmas present I've ever had. I just hope that Ramsay stays on the run for another couple of months at least.' He felt her tense and said quickly, 'Sorry! Sorry. I shouldn't have mentioned him when we're like this.'

'No, it's not that. It's just that he will probably be caught very soon now. Within a day or so, I imagine.'

'Why? How do you know?'

'Because your girlfriend has turned out to be the viper in our collective bosom.'

'What on earth are you talking about?'

'Melanie Truscott. It seems she's been in touch with Ramsay all along. He knows where we are.'

'So Mike Waters was right about her.' He glanced at Paris. 'She isn't my girlfriend; the police asked me to keep an eye on her.'

'I know; they told me. But did you have to keep such a *close* eye on her?'

'What do you mean?'

Paris lowered her head, watching her finger glide down his chest as she said in a detached tone, 'I saw you both going into her room one night.'

'Did you? And if you'd hung around for another ten minutes you would have seen me leaving.' Paris raised her eyebrows and he said, 'Melanie made some excuse about her hair-dryer not working properly. When I'd fixed it I ignored all the come-on signals and left.'

'You didn't go to bed with her?'

'No. I don't fancy Melanie, and I'm certainly not going to sleep with a woman I don't want.'

Paris smiled. 'Not even for Queen and country?'

'I'm no James Bond. I'm a one-woman man.'

'Really?' Her heart skipped a beat. 'Only one woman?'

A devilish look came into his eyes. 'Well—only one woman at a time.'

That made Paris laugh. Sitting up, she said, 'I ought to punish you for that and make you miss out a course.'

'A course?'

'Yes; because tonight is a banquet, and what you've had was just an appetiser. Now I'm going to give you the entrée—and I think you're just about ready for it.'

She moved over him, bent and kissed him until he groaned. 'Just—how many courses does this banquet have?' he gasped out.

Paris lifted her head and smiled. 'Why, just as many as you can manage.'

CHAPTER EIGHT

THE excited voices of children sounded through door panels as Paris hurried back to her own room in the morning. She could imagine them opening their presents, their eyes alight with excitement. Until last night, if she had seen children, thought of them, it would have been with guilt and sadness, but now those emotions were gone for ever, to be replaced with an exultant excitement.

She had left Will in a sleep of utter exhaustion; he had partaken deeply of his banquet, like a man starved for a long time and determined to eat his fill. And she had lured him along the way, making each time different, each course more erotic than the last, until his appetite had been sated and his strength spent.

Paris too ought to have been exhausted but had never felt more awake in her life, even though she had been carried with him to the peak of excitement many times. Her body was tired, yes, never having been loved or given so much love in one night before, but her mind was brilliantly alert, intensely happy.

For a while she sat on her bed, her chin on her knees, hugging the memory of the night to her. Later she showered and dressed, putting on a borrowed pair of tartan trews and a white cotton blouse, cinching them in with a wide black belt around her slim waist.

There were the dark shadows of a sleepless night around her eyes, but they were the radiant green of sparkling emeralds. As she fastened her hair back, Paris laughed aloud; anyone looking at her would know that she had been well and truly made love to. But would

165

they guess who by? She laughed again. As if there could possibly be anyone else but Will.

A ravenous hunger overcame her and she turned to go down to breakfast, but first she paused to look out of the window. It was a perfect Christmas Day; the snow lay thick and pristine again, but the sun was shining with that peculiarly clear luminescence of early morning out of a cloudless blue sky. Even the wind had died down. It was a golden morning.

Her thoughts went back to that first Christmas morning so long ago and she sent up a small but intense prayer for her own hopes and dreams. Then she laughed at her own lack of confidence; after last night nothing could go wrong. Life was going to be good again and she would have atoned at last.

The dining-room was already half-full of people, all of them wishing each other a merry Christmas, laughing and talking. Captain Waters had obviously kept his secret well because no one seemed to have heard about Melanie; Paris didn't hear her name mentioned once. Several people asked her how she was, whether her cold was better, and she replied that it must have been a twenty-four-hour bug, because she felt absolutely fine now.

'But you still look tired,' Mrs Paston remarked motheringly. 'You should rest for a while today. You don't want to overdo things and have to spend days in bed recovering, now do you?'

Somehow Paris managed to keep a straight face as she gravely agreed, her heart dancing inside.

None of the policemen seemed to be around this morning, which seemed strange; usually there were two or three of them having their meals at the same time as everyone else. Paris noticed but didn't think about it much. Ben came in and she waved to him. He helped himself to orange juice and porridge and came over to sit beside her.

He glanced at her face and sighed. 'Why don't the women I go to bed with look like that in the morning?'

'Never mind; you have a great way with feet, she said consolingly.

'Feet! If that's all I might as well join a monastery.'

'Don't be silly; you've just got to find the right girl. She leaned closer and lowered her voice. 'Have you heard anything more about you-know-who?'

'No. He-who-must-be-obeyed hasn't been in touch with me. Have you?'

She shook her head. 'No. What do you think is going to happen?'

Ben shrugged. 'I suppose it depends entirely on the gist of the call you-know-who made to someone-else-we-both-know.'

That made her giggle. 'What a ridiculous conversation.'

He grinned back, but said with a low forcefulness, 'I just wish to hell that it was all over and we could get away from here. Paris didn't speak and he said, 'I suppose you don't, that now you want it to go on?'

She shook her head, not even having to think about it. 'No, I want it to be over too. I have a life to get on with.'

'With Will?'

Her eyes clouded a little, lost some of their inner glow. 'It hasn't been discussed.'

'I see.'

'No, you don't. Eat your porridge.'

Allowing her to change the conversation, Ben said, 'Do you know, I'm really getting to like this stuff? I thought it tasted like wallpaper paste the first time.'

'It certainly looks like it.'

'Yes, but it grows on you.'

'Puts hairs on your chest, huh?'

He groaned, pretending to be in pain at the joke, then looked up as the waiter paused by their table. ostensibly

to give them a pot of coffee, but he also put a folded
note down beside Ben's plate. Paris reached out for the
coffee and poured it into their cups as Ben slipped the
note beneath the table and quickly read it.

'Captain Waters wants to see us in my suite immediately after breakfast.'

'Both of us?'

'That's what he says.'

She frowned. 'I wonder what he wants.'

'Just to tell us what's happening, probably. Let's keep
our fingers crossed that it's as good as over.'

They finished their breakfast and strolled out into the
hall. There was a massive pile of parcels under the
Christmas tree, in the most wonderful assortment of
shapes and sizes; they looked the sort of presents that
would intrigue a child and fill him with excitement. But
they were all to stay under the tree until after the special
lunch that was being prepared, when they would be given
out by Santa Claus, alias one of the policemen.

'Ah, Ben, I've been looking for you.' A woman came
up to him and drew him a little aside. 'We're having a
sort of talent show this evening; you will take part, won't
you? You play so well.'

Ben looked reluctant, was persuaded and profusely
thanked.

'Flattery will get you anywhere,' Paris said with irony
when he rejoined her.

'You're just jealous because you can't sing.'

They harangued each other amiably as they went up
the stairs, unaware of the glances that came their way,
and found Mike Waters already waiting for them in Ben's
suite.

'What happened last night?' Paris asked eagerly.

'Melanie made the call, as we expected,' the captain
replied. 'Only she went out by the stair on the other side
of the turret. Evidently she didn't fancy coming across
your dead body,' he said drily.

Ben, his voice sardonic, said, 'A sensitive murderess: that's something new.'

Captain Waters didn't smile; in fact he looked quite grave and Paris began to feel uneasy. 'Where is she now?' she asked.

'We took her away in the night and she's safely under lock and key. We taped her conversation. Here, I'll play it for you. You can hear Ramsay quite well because we put a minute bug in the phone, but Melanie's voice isn't that clear because of the wind. Not that she says much of any importance.'

He switched on a cassette-player and they heard the phone ringing then a man's voice say, 'Yes?'

'It's me,' Melanie replied.

'You were supposed to phone last night.'

'I couldn't. There was—there was someone around.'

'All right. Now listen. I'll come tomorrow night, Christmas night.'

'You've found where we are?'

'Yes. I've been watching the place. I can get over the outer wall all right, but I'll need you to let me in. You must be at that wine-cellar door you told me about at one in the morning, do you understand?'

'What if there's someone around?'

'Then wait till they go.' Ramsay sounded impatient. 'Use your common sense. Unlock the door earlier if you can, but I'll need you to guide me through the house.'

'What are you going to do?' Melanie's voice sounded husky, scared.

Ramsay laughed—a harsh and terrible sound that made Paris's blood run cold. 'Oh, I've got it all planned. The police have done me a favour getting everyone together; now I can deal with them all in one go.'

'What about me?'

'Don't do anything to make them suspicious. Don't pack or anything, but be ready to come with me when I leave.'

'All right. Will we really go to Spain?'

'Yes, I've said so. I've got the tickets and the false passports; there won't be any trouble. In two days we'll be there, and those bastards who put me inside will find out that I meant it when I said I'd make them pay.'

'I can't wait to see you again, Noel.'

It was difficult to understand what Melanie was saying and they realised that she must have been shivering with cold. Ramsay must have realised it too, because he cut her short and the call ended.

Ben looked grim. 'Thank God we found out in time. Now you'll be able to catch him easily. But I don't understand how he can be so confident of getting over the wall; it must be at least ten feet high.'

'It seems that Ramsay used to do some climbing in his younger days.'

'What do you think he means to do?'

The captain hesitated, and Paris said, 'I should have thought that that was pretty obvious. It sounds to me as if he intends to set fire to the place and burn us all to death.'

Ben gasped but didn't make any protest, and neither did Mike Waters try to deny it. Instead he slowly nodded and said gravely, 'I'm very much afraid you may be right.'

Ben said, 'But now you have this information you'll be able to catch him as soon as he comes within sight, so we have no need to worry. We'll all be able to sleep easy tonight.'

'It's quite possible that he'll have a gun,' Waters pointed out. 'And I don't want to run the risk of any of my men getting shot, or of Ramsay somehow getting away. So I want to take him when he comes inside.'

They both looked at him in trepidation. 'Isn't that risky?' Ben asked.

'He won't be expecting a trap.'

Paris, her voice tense, said, 'But he will be expecting Melanie to let him in. Will she do it?'

The captain shook his head. 'I couldn't risk her warning him.' Lifting his eyes, he gave Paris a direct look.

She understood at once and was immediately afraid. Her mind filled with dread; she had been unhappy for so long that she couldn't risk losing everything now, not when her dreams were within her grasp. Getting up from her chair, Paris said in great agitation, 'No. I can't. I'm sorry.'

'You'll be quite safe. My men will be all around and—'

She took a distressed step towards the door. 'No. You must get someone else.'

The captain, too, got to his feet. 'There isn't anyone else. You're the only one who knows about Melanie. The only one who—'

'Ramsay will see me. Recognise me.'

'It will be dark. And as soon as he comes inside we'll take him. You won't be in any danger. Please, Paris, for all our sakes.'

Clasping her arms defensively around herself, she shook her head vehemently. 'I'm sorry. You don't understand, but I can't—'

Her voice had risen in forceful refusal but immediately broke off as a sharp knock sounded at the door.

'You'd better answer it,' the captain said to Ben as he moved out of the line of the door. 'Get rid of whoever it is as quickly as you can.'

Ben nodded and walked over to the door, intending to open it just a few inches. But as soon as he turned the latch the door was sent crashing back on its hinges and he had to jump smartly out of the way to avoid it.

'Mind if I join the party?' Will said curtly as he strode inside. His eyes went straight to Paris standing in the middle of the room and he gave her a tight look. 'What is it you can't do?' But then he saw the captain and he frowned. 'Just what's going on?' he demanded tersely.

Captain Waters quickly shut the door. He glanced at Paris but she was standing with her hands clenched, her face pale. 'Nothing's going on. We're just having a chat, that's all.'

'Is this something to do with Melanie betraying us?' Will demanded bluntly.

Mike Waters sighed. 'How much have you told him?' he said to Paris.

'Just—just that.'

'So now you tell me the rest,' Will said in a tone so forceful that the captain didn't even try to prevaricate. Briefly he told him about the illicit phone call.

'And now he's trying to get Paris to stand in for Melanie,' Ben broke in angrily. 'I don't know how you have the nerve to ask her after all she's been through.'

Will looked at him sharply. 'What are you talking about? What happened to Paris?'

Ben looked startled. 'Didn't you tell him?' he said to her.

'No—and it's of no importance.'

Looking at Will, she suddenly thought of him lying in his bed while Ramsay stole into the building and set it on fire. She could imagine the flames leaping up the staircase, Will being trapped or overcome by smoke, the children crying and screaming in fear. The thought of them being hurt, possibly killed was quite unbearable and in the face of it her earlier refusal to help seemed small and selfish.

'I've reconsidered,' she said shortly. 'I'll do what you want.'

'But you can't!' Ben exclaimed.

'Will someone damn well tell me what's going on?' Will strode to Paris and took hold of her by the shoulders. 'What do they want you to do?'

'I told you—to take Melanie's place. To meet Ramsay and let him into the cellars,' Ben said when Paris didn't speak.

'No way.' Will turned and put himself between Paris and Captain Waters. 'I'm not going to let her do it.'

But this time the captain wasn't to be intimidated. 'Paris has already agreed. And she'll be quite safe; I've assured her of that.'

'You assured us that we would all be quite safe here until Ramsay was caught, but he fooled you into relaxing your watch on Melanie so that she was able to lead him here,' Ben said harshly. 'If he can fool you once he can fool you again.'

'No, he won't. Not this time. And it has to be Paris. I can't ask anyone else because I can't take the risk of starting a panic. If they all knew that Ramsay was near there would be uproar. I'd have all the men demanding that everyone be taken somewhere else, and all the women in hysterics. I need someone who can keep her head, the way Paris did two nights ago.'

'And just what happened two nights ago?' Will asked sharply. 'I insist that you tell me,' he said to her.

But she shook her head and it was Ben who said, 'I'll tell you. Paris saw Melanie going out onto the roof and went after her. But Melanie shut her out there in the freezing cold and left her to die.'

Will's face paled and he stared at her in appalled disbelief.

'Luckily Paris had her room key with her and she threw it through my window so I was able to go and let her in. But she couldn't have lasted much longer out there,' Ben finished.

His gaze fixed intensely on her face, Will reached out to draw her to him. 'Why didn't you tell me?' he asked, his voice unsteady.

'It was over. There was no point.' Looking into his eyes, seeing the tender anxiety in them, her heart swelled.

He'd said that when they had lived together he'd thought she'd always known that he loved her. Now she recognised that this was one of the times when there was no need for words, when his eyes said it all. She could read it now and know it for what it was; after last night she had the confidence to be sure without words.

Putting up a hand to touch her face, Will said, 'When I was outside the door I heard you say that there was something you couldn't do; was that to meet Ramsay?'

'No, of course not. It was something else entirely.'

But Ben immediately contradicted her. 'She's lying. She's scared and she doesn't really want to do it.'

Paris turned on him. 'Ben, will you please shut up? If I want to say something then I'll say it for myself. I don't need you to speak for me. I've decided to do it and that's final.'

'Oh, no, it damn well isn't,' Will said forcefully. '*I'll* let him in.'

Captain Waters soon torpedoed that idea. Giving him a scornful look, he said, 'Oh, yes, you really look like Melanie, don't you? Only about a foot taller and wider and one of the most masculine voices I've ever heard, but that doesn't matter, of course. Surely you can see that it has to be a woman?'

'Then get a policewoman to do it—someone trained to use a gun and capable of defending herself.'

'If I could, I would, but the nearest experienced woman couldn't possibly get here in time, even if I could get hold of one.'

'Then get one here by helicopter,' Will returned tersely.

'In the phone call Ramsay said that he'd been watching the place. He'd be bound to smell a rat if he saw a helicopter trying to land. Here, you'd better listen to the call for yourself.'

He switched on the cassette-player and again the menacing words filled the room.

'It doesn't take much to guess that he intends to burn the place down with all of us inside it,' Mike Waters said when it finished. 'We have to catch him—and we need Paris to help us. I've already told her that there won't be any danger.'

Both Will and Ben started to argue, but Paris said impatiently, 'Look, I've said I'll do it. You know there isn't any choice. So let's get this over and done with so that we can get on with our lives.'

'You don't *have* to do it,' Will said, coming to take her hand.

She smiled at him, but there was sadness in her eyes. 'Oh, yes, I think I have to. Don't you?'

He guessed what she meant and gave her a troubled look. 'Let's go somewhere and talk about this.'

'No.' She shook her head, afraid that he would dissuade her and that she would despise herself for being a coward forever more. 'I've made up my mind. I'm glad that you care, but this is something I have to do.'

Will looked as if he had a lot more to say, but she walked over to the door and opened it. 'It's Christmas Day; I'm going downstairs to join in the festivities. Are you coming, all of you?'

Ben came to join her but Will said, 'Shortly. I want a word with Mike first.' And he glared at the poor captain.

Downstairs there was great excitement among the children as they lined up for a fancy-dress competition on a winter and Christmas theme. The costumes, as ingenious as their parents could make them, ranged from a cotton-wool snowman to a miniature Santa Claus and a couple of delightful tree-fairies, to an amazing Christmas stocking that must have taken hours of work. This last won first prize but there was something for every child, and to Paris's amazement there was no crying or disappointment and they all behaved beautifully.

'It's all this quality time they've been having with their parents,' Ben remarked. 'They've probably never had so much attention lavished on them before in their lives.'

'You think coming here has done some good, then?'

'Must have done. And haven't you noticed how all the adults have pitched in together to think up things to pass the time? It's almost like the wartime spirit all over again.'

'How would you know about wartime spirit? You weren't even born.'

Ben grinned. 'I see I shall have to confess; I'm an old war-film groupie. I've got dozens of them on video.' He glanced at his watch. 'Would you like a pre-lunch drink?'

'Isn't it rather early?'

'Yes, but you look as if you need it.'

They went into the bar and that was where Will found them a short time later. He was looking a little grim, but his face lightened when he saw Paris. Coming over to them, he gave her a smile that was all in his eyes, that caressed and sent messages that brought last night vividly to her mind and colour to her cheeks.

Paris hastily looked away and took a sip of her drink, but Ben had noticed and said, 'I suppose you want me to go away and leave you alone?'

Will sat down with them, leaning comfortably back in the chair and crossing his legs. 'Not at all,' he said equably. 'After all, I have it on good authority that you two more than fancy each other. "Quite smitten" was the phrase the lady used when I asked where Paris was and she told me that you and Ben had gone up to his room.'

'So that was why you came charging in,' Ben said with a grin.

'It was. The dear lady didn't know whether to disapprove of your outrageous behaviour, be sentimental at the thought of you being in love, or get excited at thinking I might start a fight.'

'Who was it?'

'A gentleman never betrays a lady—even a gossip.'

Ben glanced round the bar and several curious pairs of eyes hastily turned away. He laughed. 'Well, the place would be even more boring for them without a bit of scandal.'

'Possibly. But I don't want Paris to be the cause of gossip, so to show that we're all friends I'll let you buy me a drink. A large Scotch.'

Ben went to the bar and Will said softly, 'Are you all right?'

She knew what he meant and nodded, the happiness returning to her eyes.

'You should have woken me.'

'I'm not sure I could have done; you were sleeping—very deeply.'

He grinned. 'Which is hardly surprising.' Reaching across the table, he took her hand. 'We must talk soon.'

'Tomorrow.'

'Not till then?'

'No.' She didn't want to talk about the future today, not when she had tonight hanging over her, not when she had to find the courage to face Ramsay, even if it would be for only a moment.

Will read her mind, and squeezed her hand in encouragement. Leaning forward so that only she could hear, he said, 'Don't worry, I'm not going to try and make you change your mind. I tried to persuade Waters to let me in on it, but he's refused, damn him.'

Paris gave a silent prayer of relief and deliberately sent their thoughts in another direction by saying with a coquettish look, 'You'll be adding fuel for the gossips if you talk to me this close. They'll think you're murmuring sweet nothings.'

He gave a mock leer. 'There are several very definite somethings I would like to say. And I know a very good place where I could say them this afternoon.'

'I'm shocked.'

'Is that yes or no?'

She laughed, and didn't answer as Ben came back with a tray of drinks, but made it clear in their conversation that she wanted to watch the children open their presents that afternoon. Will looked disappointed but accepted it. But for the rest of that day he left her side only when they went up to change for dinner, making it quite clear to everyone that it was he who was with her and not Ben.

It was a wonderful day; Paris enjoyed it thoroughly, especially being with Will. It was just like the old days, before she'd ruined everything, only it was better now because she had hope for the future. If the fates were kind then she would never again know the lonely emptiness of the last years. But first there was the night to face.

Will walked with her to her room just after midnight. There he kissed her long and tenderly and had to drag himself from her arms. 'Take care,' he said raggedly. 'Promise me you'll take great care.'

'I promise. You mustn't worry; I'll be fine.'

He left her and she stifled a small feeling of disappointment; she'd thought that he would have been far more emotional and encouraging, seeing what she had to face in just a short time.

Paris pushed the thought aside and changed into a black tracksuit with a hood, which Mike Waters had found for her to wear. Under it she wore a thick sweater which, it was hoped, would make her figure look more like Melanie's, and she wore her flattest shoes to make her as short as possible. It probably wouldn't fool Ramsay for more than a few minutes, but then hopefully it wouldn't even take that long before he was captured.

A policeman came for her at a quarter to one and they went down together in the service lift to the kitchens. 'Everyone's in position,' he told her. 'They're all waiting by the outside door. As soon as he walks inside, they'll take him.'

Paris nodded and took the torch he handed her as they reached the door that led down to the large cellars that ran beneath the whole building. The original owner, who'd had the house built, had been a wine buff. Now most of the basement rooms had been altered to make a space for the gymnasium and swimming pool, but there were still several rooms that held racks of wine for the hotel guests.

The door was locked. The policeman unlocked it and gave her a thumbs-up sign. 'Use the torch. Don't put on any lights. And if he makes a lunge for you shine the torch in his face.'

Paris frowned, puzzled, but nodded again. Switching on the torch, she went through the door. It closed behind her and she immediately wanted to turn and bang on the panels, to demand to be let out. For a terrible moment it was like being out on the roof all over again. Somehow she fought back the panic and went on down the steps.

She had expected it to be very cold but the central heating must have been installed here too, although it was several degrees lower than upstairs. To keep the wine at an even temperature, presumably.

Pulling the hood over her hair and forward over her face, she went on her way. Mike Waters had taken her down there earlier that day, so she knew which direction to take. Will had come with her, although the captain hadn't been very pleased. He'd pointed out the door that Ramsay would come through, shown her the wooden cases they'd stacked nearby, where the policemen would be hidden.

Now, although she walked quietly, Paris's footsteps still echoed around the corridor. It was one of the reasons why she had to do this part alone—just in case Ramsay was at a window, watching, listening. If he heard two sets of footsteps he would immediately take alarm and they might lose him again.

The corridor came to an end. To reach the outer door, she now had to unlock another door and go through a series of cellars, first passing rooms that had once been used as laundries, lamp-room, boot-room—all the workplaces that had been needed when the castle had been a private house and which now were largely obsolete.

There was time yet and it wasn't easy walking by the light of the torch, but she went as quickly as she could. There was a faint noise and her scalp prickled, her heart standing still for a moment, but the noise didn't come again and she thought of mice. Lord, she was scared to death of mice.

One of the doors, marked mysteriously 'Fish-Room', stood open. Paris went to walk past it and caught a definite whiff of tobacco smoke. Was one of the policemen hiding there? She took another step and then a low voice said, 'Melanie.'

She froze, then swung round. And there, in the light of the torch, grinning at her, stood Noel Ramsay.

He put up an arm to shield his face from the light. 'Don't shine it on me. Here, give it to me and let me look at you.'

Paris instantly turned off the torch and threw it as far away as possible. Then she raised her voice to a squeal that wasn't far short of a scream, praying that the police would hear. 'You frightened me!'

'Sorry, darling.' But he didn't sound it. 'Where's the torch?'

Trying to make her voice as nasal as possible, Paris said, 'You gave me such a start, I dropped it.'

'Damn!'

She felt him grope for her and he found her arm and held it before she could move away. Without warning he pulled her into his arms and kissed her. There was no finesse about it; he pressed his mouth hard against her own, bruising her lips, at the same time taking her breast in his hand and squeezing. He had grown a beard and it felt like wire on her skin.

'There, that's what you've been missing. And there's plenty more to come.' He laughed, plainly pleased with himself.

He let go of one of her arms and Paris rubbed her hand across her mouth, feeling ill. She wanted to wrench herself away from him, to run back towards the light and warmth and peacefulness of the hotel, but she knew that somehow she must let the police know that he was already inside.

'Why aren't you waiting by the door, like we said? How did you get in?'

His hand tightened a little. 'Your voice sounds different.'

Trying desperately to sound like Melanie, Paris said in an accusing tone, 'I caught a cold out on the roof, calling you.'

'Now she tells me,' Ramsay said in distaste. But he let her go, saying, 'Search around; see if you can find the torch.'

'Was the door open already?'

'No, but I got here early and it was too damn cold to wait outside, so I broke a window and got in that way. I would have tried to get up to your room and surprise you there if the door out of here hadn't been locked. Then I could have given you what you really want, couldn't I, my sweet?' he said lasciviously.

Paris shuddered but managed a pretty good attempt at a coquettish giggle. 'We'd better go along to the door, make sure it's unlocked and ready for us to get away quick.'

But Ramsay said, 'There's no point; we can get out of any door. Have you found the torch?'

'No. It must have rolled.'

'You should have had enough sense to hold onto it.'

'You made me jump,' she responded in an aggrieved tone. She had found the wall of the corridor and was moving along it in the direction of the outer door, raising her voice, desperately hoping that the sound would carry and someone would hear.

'Where are you going?'

'I'm looking for the torch.'

'Forget it. Did you leave the door you came through open?'

'Yes. And the one in the kitchen that leads down here,' Paris said without thinking.

Ramsay's voice filled with satisfaction. 'Good. Come here. We can find our way up; my eyes have got used to the dark now.'

Paris's hand felt something on the wall and she realised it was a light switch; hastily she moved her hand away; the last thing she wanted now was light. In the distance she thought she heard a noise, very soft, but it sent a wave of hope to her heart. To cover it, afraid that Ramsay might also have heard it, she said loudly, 'What about the torch? It must be round here somewhere.'

His voice sharpened. 'I said forget it. Come over here.'

Perhaps he had heard or had become suspicious of her voice again. To lull him, praying that the noise wasn't just mice, Paris said, 'Have you got the passports, like you said? How will we get to Spain?'

'Don't worry about that; it's all taken care of. Come here, darling.'

There was no help for it; he would become really suspicious if she didn't do what he wanted. With an inner sob, Paris turned and groped her way back to him. 'Here I am.'

'That's my girl. You sure those doors are unlocked?'

'Yes, I've said so, haven't I?'

'Just making sure.' Suddenly he laughed, the sound echoing horribly in the darkness. 'Just making sure I don't need you any more, you silly cow. Do you really think I'd take a cheap tart like you with me? No, you gave evidence against me and you're going to die with the rest of them.'

She tried to pull away but he grabbed her and held her close against him, so that she could smell the stink of tobacco and drink on his breath, the unwashed odour of his skin.

'And you'll be the first to go, and you'll know what's coming to you. You'll—'

His voice broke off with a gasp as she brought her knee up as hard as she could. He let go of one of her arms and she hit him in the face, wrenching herself free and turning to run blindly along the corridor towards the police, screaming for help as she went.

Behind her Ramsay gave a grunt and then she heard his footsteps pounding after her. Her outstretched hand brushed a wall and she guessed that she must have gone through the archway into the first of the wine cellars. If she could only hide! She turned to her left, hoping to find the wine racks, but tripped over something on the floor and went crashing down.

It must have been a barrel; it went skittering across the floor and landed against another rack. There was light! She gave a moan of thankfulness, thinking that it must be the police at last, but then realised that it was coming from behind her.

The light flickered and grew brighter as Ramsay came nearer, and she realised that he must have a cigarette lighter. Paris was leaning against a wine rack and hastily used it to pull herself to her feet as he came into the cellar. He laughed when he saw her, enjoying himself, knowing that she was trapped, but swore when she grabbed a bottle and turned to throw it at him.

He ducked and the lighter went out, plunging them into even deeper darkness. With a terrified sob, Paris pulled out more bottles and hurled them in his direction. Suddenly he was on her and she screamed again. Desperately she hit out, trying to break free, but he was so strong, so strong. His hands went to her throat and he began to squeeze. His laugh filled her ears as the blackness began to grow even deeper.

Suddenly there was light again—the dark-destroying glare of a powerful electric bulb. The grip on her throat relaxed as Ramsay reacted with surprise. Paris opened her eyes and looked into his startled eyes as he saw her face for the first time. Then a hand caught his shoulder and he was wrenched away from her as Will's voice said, 'Try fighting a man instead of a woman, you murdering swine.'

Putting her hands up to her throat, Paris leaned limply against the wine rack and watched. Ramsay, knowing that he had walked into a trap, fought desperately and dirty. But Will was in a cold, implacable rage. Though the two men were of similar height and build it was obvious from the start that Ramsay didn't stand a chance. A lot of hard blows were exchanged but then Will hit him good and hard, and when Ramsay, knowing that he was beaten, tried to get a revolver from his pocket Will just smashed his hand against the wall until he dropped it.

Paris became aware that the police were there, that Captain Waters was trying to stop the fight, but Will pushed him out of the way too and went on grimly hitting Ramsay until he fell to the ground.

Then Will stood there, legs braced, chest heaving, hands still clenched into bruised fists, staring down at their enemy, almost as if daring him to get up so that

he could hit him again. Only when the captain stooped
to put handcuffs on Ramsay did Will straighten up, then
stride over to take Paris in his arms.

'How did you get here? Oh, how did you get here?'
she said with a sob, her head against his shoulder.

'Did you really think I'd let you come down here
alone? Never in a million years.'

Will insisted on carrying her up to her room and would
have stayed with her, but his face was bruised and
bleeding and she insisted he be attended to, asking instead for Mrs Paston to come and sit with her. The older
lady came bustling in wearing a quilted red dressing gown
and held Paris's hand for the rest of the night.

Tomorrow everyone would be told that Ramsay had
been caught and that they were free to go, but only a
few would ever know just how close he had come to
gaining his revenge.

Early in the morning, before anyone else was about, Paris
dressed and packed what was left of her clothes, then
went to find Captain Waters. He wouldn't agree to what
she wanted at first, but she was adamant, and shortly
afterwards Paris climbed into a Range Rover that drove
her away.

As they went through the gatehouse archway, Paris
glanced back at the castle. So much had happened there,
both unbelievably good as well as indescribably terrible.
Somehow she must try to forget the bad and remember
only the good. There was the future to look forward to
now and she was full of hope.

They went through the archway and the building was
lost from sight. She had done everything she could to
atone; now she must wait and see if she had been forgiven and fate would be kind to her.

The daffodils were in bud before Will found her. Paris
had bought some from the local market along with a

basket of groceries. It was Saturday and the sun was shining, bringing the first promise of spring.

She had got over the trauma of Ramsay's attack and no longer woke in shuddering fear as she went through it in her dreams. Now she knew an inner contentment and was able to face the world on equal terms again.

Will was waiting outside her building, leaning against his car and reading a newspaper. He saw her first and tossed the paper through the window of the car, then walked purposefully to meet her. Paris stood still, her heart giving a great leap of thankfulness. When he came up to her, they just stood and gazed at each other for long minutes. There was a guarded look about Will's eyes and he didn't attempt to kiss her.

Reaching down, he took her basket from her. 'You have been extremely difficult to track down,' he commented as he fell into step beside her.

'Have I?' Her voice was unsteady.

'You're not in the phone book, your company refused to give me your address, and Captain Waters wouldn't tell me it even when I threatened to spill the beans on his cock-up over catching Ramsay. In the end I had to go through all the electoral registers for most of London before I found you. And then, of course, you weren't here. "Gone abroad," your neighbour said.'

They reached the entrance to the building. Paris punched in her code number, they went inside and took the lift to her floor. Once inside the flat, Will at last took her in his arms and kissed her.

When he finally raised his head, he said raggedly, 'Are you going to go on disappearing from my life, making me go through hell until I find you? Because I warn you, Paris, I don't think I can take it again.'

'You—you can't?'

'No, I think it would be much better if we got married so that I can tie you down if necessary.'

She smiled but said, 'Is that why you want to marry me, then?'

His arms tightened around her and he looked down at her with intense tenderness. 'No, you idiot, it's because I love you most dearly, and because I know I can't live without you. And we'll do it on your terms, have it any way you want.'

She knew that he was referring to her work and loved him the more for it, but it was incidental now. 'I've waited a long time to hear you say that,' she said huskily.

Drawing a little away from her, Will gave her a searching look. 'Why did you leave the castle so soon, without seeing me? I went searching for you but Mike Waters said you'd insisted on leaving.'

Paris moved away a few steps, then turned to face him again. 'It was so that—this could happen. I wanted you to be sure that you really loved me, that you'd forgiven me. I knew that if you came to find me then you would still care, that the past would no longer be between us.'

'It isn't,' he said instantly. 'And I was as much to blame; I've realised that now. If you'd been confident of my feelings for you, you would have come to me instead of Emma. I let you down when you needed me, and it never occurred to me that you might have done it for my sake. I think it was the fact that you hadn't told me, that I'd had to learn it from someone else that made me go over the top and react the way I did. I was a damn fool not to listen to you then; I wasted those years when we could have been together.'

'Yes, you should have listened,' she agreed. 'Because I never had an abortion.'

He stared at her. 'But I don't understand.'

'I'd decided to keep the baby, but I had an accident. Oh, nothing major,' she added as he gave her a startled look. 'Just a fall, but I lost it. I should have told you, I know, but I wanted everything to be the same between us. But it couldn't be, because I felt so guilty.'

'But if it wasn't your fault...'

She swung away from him. 'But I'd thought about an abortion, considered it as an option. And when I had the miscarriage—' her voice filled with pain '—I wasn't altogether sorry, because I'd been so afraid of losing you.'

'Oh, Paris,' Will said wretchedly. 'Why didn't you tell me this when we were at the castle?'

Turning to face him, she said, 'Would you have believed me? Every time I saw you, you threw the abortion in my face. You were still so angry—' She broke off, biting her lip.

'I'm sorry. I'm so sorry.' Reaching for her, he said urgently, 'Will *you* forgive *me*, my love?'

'There's nothing to forgive.' Lifting her hands to either side of his face, Paris gazed at him for a long moment, her eyes alight with happiness. 'I love you—love you with all my heart.' Then she reached to gently kiss his lips.

'And I you,' he said softly. 'I shall go on telling you that for the rest of my life.' His expression changed. 'That's if you ever get round to saying yes, of course.'

Paris dropped her eyes, took a step away from him.

Something in her manner made Will say sharply, 'What is it?'

'There—there's something you ought to know.' Lifting her head, she looked at him directly, her gaze serious. 'I lied to you.'

His face set, grew tense, as if expecting a blow. 'Lied? How?'

'That night we spent together at the castle, you asked me if I was protected. Well, I wasn't.'

Will stared at her, his face slowly changing as he realised. 'You mean, you...?'

Paris nodded, imps of happy devilment in her eyes. 'Yes, if you marry me you'll have to take on our child as well.'

He gave a disbelieving shake of his head. 'But this is—wonderful! Incredible! But what about your career?'

'Maybe I'll put that on hold for a while.'

Catching hold of her hands, he held them tightly. 'Are you sure?'

'Oh, yes, I've seen a doctor.'

'No. I meant, are you sure this is what you want? Why did you do it? What if I hadn't come to find you?'

'It wouldn't have made any difference. I knew that this was the only way I could atone for what happened, and I want this baby—want it desperately Almost as much as I want you,' she added softly.

Putting his arms round her, Will gave her an exuberant hug, sweeping her off her feet, a huge grin on his face. 'I'm going to be a father! Can you beat that?' Then he set her on her feet and said, 'Don't just stand there; we've got to go out and find a house for the three of us.' Taking her hand, he pulled her towards the door, then stopped. 'You still haven't said it,' he complained.

Paris laughed. 'Well, OK, I suppose I'd better make an honest man of you.'

'Is that the best you can do?'

Her voice softened. 'No—the best is yet to come, my love ...'

MILLS & BOON®

Christmas
Miracles

Christmas Miracles really can happen, as you'll
find out in our festive collection of three
heart-warming romantic stories from three of
our most popular authors:

A Christmas Proposal ★ by **Betty Neels**

Heavenly Angels ★ by **Carole Mortimer**

A Daddy for Christmas ★ by **Rebecca Winters**

Available: November '96   Price: £4.99

MILLS & BOON®

November's Romances

♡

Each month you can choose from a wide variety of romance with Mills & Boon. Below are the new titles to look out for next month in our two new series Presents and Enchanted.

Presents™

ONE-MAN WOMAN	Carole Mortimer
MEANT TO MARRY	Robyn Donald
AUNT LUCY'S LOVER	Miranda Lee
HIS SLEEPING PARTNER	Elizabeth Oldfield
DOMINIC'S CHILD	Catherine Spencer
JILTED BRIDE	Elizabeth Power
LIVING WITH THE ENEMY	Laura Martin
THE TROPHY WIFE	Rosalie Ash

Enchanted™

NO MORE SECRETS	Catherine George
DADDY'S LITTLE HELPER	Debbie Macomber
ONCE BURNED	Margaret Way
REBEL IN DISGUISE	Lucy Gordon
FIRST-TIME FATHER	Emma Richmond
HONEYMOON ASSIGNMENT	Sally Carr
WHERE THERE'S A WILL	Day Leclaire
DESERT WEDDING	Alexandra Scott

Available from WH Smith, John Menzies, Volume One, Forbuoys, Martins, Woolworths, Tesco, Asda, Safeway and other paperback stockists.

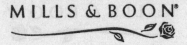

MILLS & BOON®

December's Romances

Each month you can choose from a wide variety of romance with Mills & Boon. Below are the new titles to look out for next month in our two new series Presents and Enchanted.

Presents™

THEIR WEDDING DAY	Emma Darcy
THE FINAL PROPOSAL	Robyn Donald
HIS BABY!	Sharon Kendrick
MARRIED FOR REAL	Lindsay Armstrong
MISTLETOE MAN	Kathleen O'Brien
BAD INFLUENCE	Susanne McCarthy
TORN BY DESIRE	Natalie Fox
POWERFUL PERSUASION	Margaret Mayo

Enchanted™

THE VICAR'S DAUGHTER	Betty Neels
BECAUSE OF THE BABY	Debbie Macomber
UNEXPECTED ENGAGEMENT	Jessica Steele
BORROWED WIFE	Patricia Wilson
ANGEL BRIDE	Barbara McMahon
A WIFE FOR CHRISTMAS	Pamela Bauer & Judy Kaye
ALL SHE WANTS FOR CHRISTMAS	Liz Fielding
TROUBLE IN PARADISE	Grace Green